THE SCENT OF
SOMETHING SNEAKY

For further information, contact:
Tumblehome Learning, Inc.
P.O. Box 171386
Boston, MA 02117, USA
http://www.tumblehomelearning.com

Library of Congress Control Number: 2015944989

Hedrick, Gail E.
THE SCENT OF SOMETHING SNEAKY / Gail E. Hedrick - 1st ed

ISBN 978-0-9897924-8-6
1. Children - Fiction 2. Science Fiction 3. Mystery

Cover art/design: Barnas Monteith

Printed in Canada

10 9 8 7 6 5 4 3 2 1

THE SCENT OF
SOMETHING SNEAKY

By Gail E. Hedrick

Tumblehome l e a r n i n g, Inc.

For our grandson,
Callum,
who already loves books
almost as much as I love him.

TABLE OF CONTENTS

Chapter 1

The Summer Begins

I rolled over, snuggled deeper under the covers and scrunched my eyes a little tighter to keep out the sunrise trying to nudge me awake. Ah, a few more blissful moments. Then I caught the aroma of coffee drifting up from downstairs. I don't drink coffee yet, but I love figuring out smells; they intrigue me. I sniffed again. Hmm, was that hazelnut or toasted almond? I itched to know, but not enough to leave my warm, cozy bed. Then came a scream . . . not a yell, not a holler, but a woman's scream of distress. It didn't sound like Mom.

I bolted awake, remembering I was at Baird's Den, the North Carolina bed and breakfast where I'd be working the rest of the summer. I had come to help fill in for the husband and wife team who were normally here. I tugged on my bunny slippers and ran out into the hall in my pajamas. Not stopping for one second, I nearly slid down the back stairs to the empty kitchen. Looking outside, I saw a man sprawled on the grass, bleeding from a cut on his head. My friend, Mary Carnell, dabbed futilely at the blood with a tissue. Her grandmother, Gigi Baird, who owned the inn, spoke into a cell phone, gesturing with her free hand. I guessed she was talking to 911.

I grabbed two dishtowels from their hooks, headed out across the back porch, leaped over a hole where a step should have been, and landed on the grass. I knelt down beside the man, and motioned for Mary to do the same thing on his other side. She was strangely dressed, totally in orange, which for me was too peppy this early in the morning. Forcing myself to focus, I folded one of the towels into a small square, pressed it over the cut, and pushed Mary's hand on top of it. I tied the other towel around the man's head to hold the makeshift bandage in place.

Mary slid her hand free, blew out a huge breath, and looked at him. "Mr. Blanton, this is Emily Sanders, one of our summer helpers who, thank goodness, apparently knows first aid."

I shrugged. "Junior lifeguard training. Pleased to meet you, sir."

"Same here." Glancing over, he said, "My four-year-old has those same slippers." He touched the towel and winced. "Seriously, thanks for what you did."

I nodded, smiled, and tried to act like everyone administered first aid in pajamas. Embarrassing? Oh, yessss.

Mary glanced at my feet, took in the rest of my "outfit," and shook her head. "Em, Mr. Blanton's a sales rep and stays here on business trips."

"It's a nice place," I said, checking the bandage. "Sir, does your neck hurt?"

Mr. Blanton gave me a small nod.

"Ah, maybe you should stay lying down for a bit," I suggested. "So, you fell, sir?"

He squinted as if he was forcing himself to think. "Well, I'm not sure. One minute I was cooling down after a run, and the next? Wham, I'm on the ground!"

Gigi clicked off the phone. "EMS is on the way." She pointed at the back step board, which now sat in one of the planters beside the porch as if it had crash-landed in the petunias. "Goodness, I was at the sink peering out the open window. I saw Jay and reminded him he was a 'back-door-worthy' guest, so he turned around to come in the way we do, through the kitchen. But, the moment he put his foot on the left end of the step, the whole board flipped up, and down he went, sideways." She squatted and patted his arm. "I think your head hit the corner of one of the flowerboxes."

"It got him pretty good," I said, looking toward the street. "Wow, is that the ambulance already? That was quick."

Mary looked at Mr. Blanton, and sniffed as a big tear rolled down her cheek. "Gram, I wish we could have done more, I'm so sorry."

"Hush, now," said Gigi. "Not many places have *grown-ups* working for them who would be such a big help, let alone fourteen-year-olds. But now that the ambulance is here, why don't you head back inside to check on things? Emily, you may want to change out of those pajamas. I'll stay right here." She turned to Mr. Blanton. "Hopefully, the hospital won't keep you long, and you'll be back here for the bedtime snack."

As we headed inside, Mary nudged me. "How was this as a start to your first morning?"

I grabbed my waistband. "Okay, forget the slippers. I'm dying that I administered first aid to a guest in my pajamas. Who does that? I can't believe Gigi was so calm about it. I'm so mortified."

"Whoa, Gram *is* pretty calm about stuff. She'd heard you were my fearless friend, ready to jump in where needed. That trait worked well for us today."

I took a super deep breath. "Thanks. This morning was crazy. Is it like this all the time?"

Mary yanked her orange-striped headband off. She had to hold her hair back when cooking for the inn. Her brown crayon-colored hair was growing out from an unfortunate haircut she gave herself to honor Joan of Arc day at our school. Tucking a strand behind her ears, she said, "On a normal morning while I'm serving up yummy plates of food, someone says 'Oh, I'd like another glass of juice,' not 'Help, I'm bleeding.' This whole thing freaked me out."

I held up my fist. "That's why you called me. No worries. As long as it doesn't involve me making a soufflé, I'm here to help ya. Work hard, play hard. That's what you told me on the phone."

"I did say that." Mary frowned. "So, roomie, don't you run out on me, you hear?"

I shrugged. "Let's not go crazy, because you may have fed the guests, but you haven't fed *me*, and the verdict is still out on whether two peas crammed in that little peapod room will work. If you use many more hangers, you may have to get a room down the street at the Smith Family Motel."

"Okay on the hangers," she said, grinning. "And we're the staff until Mr. and Mrs. Beck get back from their sabbatical, so forage around in the kitchen on your own. We serve breakfast daily from seven to nine, and staff gets all the leftovers. Today, there should still be some raisin bread, pancakes, bacon and OJ or fruit."

Yum, I was ravenous. I headed in the direction of food, then looked back. "Your grandma's moving around better than I expected."

Mary nodded. "When I first got here, she couldn't make it up the stairs, so we had a bed in the office. She's way better. I'm glad, cuz she's also pretty cool, yes?"

"For sure. She's not an 'old lady' kind of grandma. Cute hair, great L.L. Bean clothes. When did you decide to stay the whole summer?"

Mary tapped her chest. "*I* didn't. I was only supposed to come up for a few weeks while my parents were second honeymooning in France. When Gram had that fall, it was like, well Mary can just stay as long as you need her."

"Wow, not the summer you planned, right?"

"Nope," agreed Mary, "but the truth is, it's not out of character for my parents. Mom's starting her latest romance novel, and my dad's deadline on a new sculpture got moved up. They just didn't want me underfoot."

Hmm, I thought, the downside of having famous, creative parents. I wanted to be more independent of my parents, who practically cried as they left me off here the other day, but I truly couldn't imagine basically being shoved out the door like Mary. "I'm sorry."

Mary shrugged. "I'm kind of used to it. And, sometimes they send me good gifts. Anyway, I called you because the inn was still too much for just Gram and me. You became our saving grace."

I tilted my head toward the kitchen, and didn't reply. Was I glad I'd said yes? This was a beautiful inn, but really, what had I gotten myself into? It had sounded so fun, but after our little staff meeting last night, I realized we had no control over our own time, serious stuff could happen like picky guests or now blood, we'd probably have to dress nicely most of the time, and since I was the maid, my job involved a lot of ick. Then, our schedules were so crazy, how could I plan my workouts, and practice for swim team? Plus, if I was homesick for Virginia after only fifteen hours, would that get better? Had I made a really dumb decision to come up here? All I'd heard was "you'll make enough money to finally get your own cell phone," and I hadn't thought about anything else.

I munched a second (or was it a third?) yummy piece of bacon and eyed the phone, considering a call home to mom to come get me. The problem was, I'd worked so hard to convince my parents to let me do this, it would be embarrassing to admit defeat this soon. Finishing my OJ, I made a decision. I'd give this place a week. If I hadn't gotten eaten by a bear or fired (what was I thinking charging outside in pajamas?) I'd decide then if I should stay or run back home.

Chapter 2

Private Stuff, Public House

Later, I followed the sound of voices down the stairs and heard Gigi say, "Let's plan to have today's breakfast again next Sunday. Those peach pancakes were terrific."

Aha! Knowing Mary, I realized her outfit was not actually orange. My friend was a really good artist who could paint, draw, and most recently do collage. It didn't matter what, she was pretty amazing. But, as a by-product, she loved to "immerse herself in her art." Instead of a breakfast special being just food, for Mary peach pancakes meant dressing head to toe in peachy shades of orange. I grinned to myself and pushed open the swinging door to the kitchen.

Gigi waved me over to the big wood-topped center island, pointed for me to sit on the barstool beside hers, and gave me a hug. "Good job today, young lady!"

I shook my head. "Thanks. My whole body started quivering about the second the ambulance drove off."

"Rush of adrenaline, I bet. But you were cool when it counted," declared Gigi. "The EMS guys said your bandage got no points for style, but the pressure amount was just right."

"Cool," I said. "Does Mr. Blanton have some family we should call?"

"Already did it," nodded Gigi. "He was conscious as they left, and the EMS crew said they wouldn't run the siren so he could speak to his wife when she called. They also said they'd complete an accident report which goes to the sheriff and the state inspector."

"Inspector?" I asked.

"Oh, sweetie," said Gigi, shoving a hand through her short, layered hair, the color of molasses with wisps of blonde. Not a granny image at all. She might not be back at full strength, but her hiking shorts, trail shirt, and rugged sandals showed she knew her way around the mountains. "Inn owners get inspected periodically, so I expect someone official-looking here in a couple days. It's good, and weeds out the shoddily run B&Bs, but we never know what they'll notice."

"Well, they shouldn't find anything," grumbled Mary. "This place is beautiful. And it doesn't make sense because we use those steps a bunch. You'll get to know them well, Em, cuz that's how you get to the inn's dumpster, or as we fondly call it, the bears' buffet."

"How do you mean that? You mean bears come in groups?" I gasped. "The inn's brochure says the 'occasional' bear."

Gigi gave Mary a look over her glasses, and then patted my arm. "We actually do have bears up here, but so far this summer, not many sightings."

"Which still means more than one, yes?"

"True," agreed Gigi, "but none near here. The reason Mary blurted that out is, they love to root around looking for food scraps, so it's imperative to keep the dumpster gate shut tight so they can't get into it and have the buffet."

"I can do that," I said. Hey, I knew there were bears in the mountains. I just thought that meant *on* a mountain, not ambling down a street. "I'll be the best gate-closer you ever saw."

"I never doubted it for a moment," said Gigi. "Mary, I know what you mean about the steps, but an insurance company won't care. They see negligence and liability issues, which means dollar signs. I've left messages for my agent and our attorney. They probably won't call today, as it is still Sunday, after all. I took photos of everything, and my camera is in the office. If we get a call about Jay Blanton, please come get me." She put both hands on the counter and bit her lip as she pushed up off the stool.

"I need to stretch out before the next batch of guests arrives. Until I can get the step fixed, could y'all see about blocking that area off? There should be sawhorses and rope in the carriage house."

"Sure," said Mary, holding up her arms to show off her muscles. "We'll take care of it."

Gigi lightly tapped her on the head. "See, girls? I needed you and here you are." She went up the back stairs, looking like she was carrying the whole weight of this 105-year-old inn on her shoulders.

~

Mary headed for the phone ringing in the office, and I started out back toward the carriage house. As I got to the door, there was a knock on the other side. Hmm, would this be a lost guest? There was never much hope for my short red hair, but I fluffed the curls anyway and opened the door. There stood someone who did not at all resemble a guest, but still was really cute. "Hi, may I help you?"

A slender, athletic boy held up his grubby hands. "Nah, I wanted to wash up or maybe even jump in one of the showers."

"Not a chance—the showers are spotless. Is it normal for people in Winton to randomly drop by to take a shower?"

He grinned and shoved his baseball cap back a bit. Shiny black hair peeked out around the edge of the hat. "I'm not sure about 'people' but most places have *some* perks for employees. I'm Alex Ortiz, Baird's Den lawn guy. I need to get this weed stuff off my hands. I was down the street doing the Landon place, and I'm killing some time till they get home. Then I'll go back and get paid. So, if not the shower, how about the kitchen sink?"

I looked at his stained tennis shoes and the grass clippings stuck to his arms, then opened the door wide. "Well, your clothes match your story, so come in. I'm Emily Sanders, Baird's Den summer cleaning girl. Let me see if I can find some towels."

"No sweat, I've got this." Alex headed for the sink and reached underneath for soap and a couple towels. "Hey, did I see an ambulance come this way?"

I nodded. "Yeah, it was pretty crazy for awhile. A guest fell out back."

"Ah, that probably explains the gap in the steps." Alex turned his head toward me, careful to leave his hands dripping over the sink. "Just so you know, I grew up two streets over and generally slide in the back door. I usually wait on myself, but didn't want to freak anyone out if Ms. Gigi wasn't around."

"Okay," I said, shrugging. "You won't bother me."

Alex dried his hands. "Good, then you won't mind if I get some water."

"Nope, help yourself."

And he did. Plus, he lifted the head of a big ceramic bear and peeked in, then reached in and came out with a palm-sized cookie. He sniffed it, grinned, and said, "Only chocolate chip one I've ever had like my grandmother's. Ask Ms. Gigi about the secret ingredient."

I nodded, thinking he really was comfy around here. Mary was still on the phone, and it sounded like a complicated reservation, so I decided not to wait. "If you want to hang out, Mary should be done soon. We're supposed to block the steps with some sawhorses, so I'm going to go find them."

Alex shook his head. "That's tricky if you don't know the carriage house. I'd better show you around."

"Okay," I said. "We also need rope and some rags. Anything like that out there?"

He grabbed the door and motioned for me go first. "Yeah, the joke here is, if you can't find it, look in the carriage house." Outside, he glanced down at the step board and empty space where it should have been. "Crazy how that came loose."

We slid open the big garage-type doors of the carriage house. Right in front were two lawn mowers, some rakes, and a slew of shovels. Bags of potting soil and fertilizer were stacked on wooden storage racks. Rope of all sizes hung in loops on the wall studs, and there was a basket of rags on one of the workbenches. It looked as if *Southern Living* magazine had exploded in this building, leaving all its contents behind, both practical and pretty.

Off to the side was one bench that didn't really match anything else. A stool sat in front of it, and stashed on the bench top stood what looked like specimen jars, several wooden shadowboxes with glass fronts housing butterfly collections, and of all things, a microscope. "What's that stuff for?"

He glanced in that direction and sighed. "That was Ms. Gigi's husband, Mr. Lionel's area, his workstation. He was an amateur naturalist, and spent a lot of time out here. Everybody misses him, he was a good guy."

Alex headed toward the back of the structure, reached into a closet area, and dragged out two sawhorses. "We have more up in the loft, but two's probably enough. I'll get these. You grab some rope and rags. I assume you want to attach the rags to the rope like flags?"

I nodded, thinking he looked like a teenager but sounded like a grown-up, all practical, organized and kind of bossy. We loaded up and hauled everything to the sidewalk by the back porch. The steps were generously wide, with space enough that all three of us kids could have sat beside each other. It took some shoving and rearranging around the steps a couple times, but pretty soon, we had a serious-looking warning area going.

"We could just tie the rags on the rope themselves," he said, "but if we cut the rags, we wouldn't have to use so many."

"Yeah," I said, "good idea. What are you, like in tenth?"

"No, I'll be at the high school, but in ninth." He looked around. "I need scissors."

I grinned. "What, no pocket knife?"

His cheeks flamed with a red glow. He didn't blush like I did, as his skin was so brown, but it was definitely a blush. "Yeah, I get accused of always being prepared. Guess I slacked off today."

These rags were super clean, so I put one between my teeth and tore a little ways down. Then I tugged each side of the rag and ripped it in two pieces. I went "tah-dah," but Alex just shrugged. Anyway, soon we had a platoon of rags dangling from the rope around the sawhorses.

We talked for a few minutes, then both turned as Mary peeked her head around the doorjamb. "Hola, guy."

"Hola, chica," grinned Alex. He looked at me. "My mom and grandma were born in Mexico, and this one likes to practice her Spanish on me."

Mary wrinkled her nose, and said, "Yeah, he's hard to keep up with, but no worries with Emily. She takes Latin."

"Ah," said Alex, "a brainy one."

"Sometimes." I pointed to the sawhorses. "Well?"

"Looks good," Mary said.

Alex cleared his throat. "Hey, I can probably fix the step."

"Heck," said Mary. "I'm surprised you don't have some tools out here already."

"Well, I didn't come here to do work," he said, getting down on his hands and knees on the porch. "I just came by to wash up."

"And steal a cookie," I pointed out.

"Always," he said, peeking up at Mary. "I can handle this, no prob."

Mary tapped his baseball hat, and looked at me. "This one knows bunches about wood, trees, and saws. He made that little chair in our room."

"Nice. So, we break something this summer, you can fix?"

"Well, not everything." He slid off the porch and studied the planter box. "Hmm, one of the corners of this is cracked."

"Yeah," I said, "that's where Mr. Blanton hit his head."

"Was he hurt bad?"

I shook my head. "There was a pretty deep cut, but otherwise I think he's okay."

Alex stared at us. "So what happened?"

"Well," said Mary, "Gram invited him to come in the back door like we always do. It sounded like he sort of came from the side, like he'd just turned around and started up." She handed me the board to put it back in the spot so I could demonstrate what might have happened.

"Hmm, I'm not sure where the last nail is, but look. These nails on the left end of the board are a little bent now, but they match up perfectly with the holes in this support thingy." I lined up the nails and the holes on the left end of the board toward the driveway where Mr. Blanton had come from. Then, I pushed the board back into place. "You can see nail holes but no nails holding the other end down. I'm not sure why they're missing. All the other steps have nails at both ends. Anyway, here's the step board looking almost like normal, and I'm Mr. Blanton." I pushed down on the far left end of the step board, beyond the nails, the way someone's foot would, and the other end flew up toward the sky. "Instead of a step, we have a lever, yes?"

"Looks like one," agreed Mary.

"And dangerous," Alex said grimly. "I'll take care of it. But you'll need a carpenter to fix the planter, because I don't have a miter box to make the angles."

I laughed. "Aw, the wood-guy failed the test."

"Well, maybe," Alex said, looking first at me, then Mary. He reached down beside his foot. "At least I can save Ms. Gigi some money."

"What?" asked Mary.

Alex held his hand up to us, and waved a fairly straight, slightly rusted nail.

I picked up the step board. "Wait, did that come from the loose end of the step?"

Alex nodded. "Well, it matches the others."

I said, "Well, that won't save her much money—you need more, right?"

"Wait one minute." He searched both sides of the steps, then went across the porch and jumped down on the right side by the other planter. He motioned for us to look down where he was standing. Resting in the dirt beside the planter lay more nails. "I spread pine straw the other day in all the planters, and I saw something on the ground, but I was trying to get done and didn't go back to check. I feel bad now that I didn't."

"You mean the nails were out of the step for days?" I asked.

"They could have been," said Alex. "As long as someone steps on the middle, nothing happens. It only flips when someone steps on the end."

"Well, don't beat yourself up," insisted Mary.

"Right," I said. "But how'd they pop out and end up over here?"

"This is pressure-treated wood," said Alex, reminding me of a teacher. "When they first treat it, it's full of water. As it dries, it shrinks. Sometimes nails have to be hammered down again."

"So, if they weren't hammered down," Mary asked, "these could have worked loose on their own?"

"Actually, it happens a lot," said Alex.

I squinted, and then nodded. "Yeah, but I see a dent in the wood. You can see it pretty well if you tilt it a little."

Mary looked at me like I was crazy. "What would that mean?"

I shrugged. "I've used a hammer a lot." I pointed at the nails. "I think it means the nails were pried out with the claw end of a hammer."

"Whoa," said Alex. "Hammer claws make deep gouges, not like these faint marks."

I scrunched up my face. "Okay, then no matter how they came out, why or how would they have wound up so near each other? That seems really weird."

"Maybe it was the carpenter," Mary suggested. "Like the nails were duds, he threw them down, and he just forgot about 'em."

"It's possible," Alex agreed. "Remember, we can't be sure these nails were from *this* step."

"Maybe this whole deal was a summer prank," I offered.

Mary frowned. "You mean like kids?"

I tapped the step with my sneaker. "Or maybe someone wanted to hurt Mr. Blanton."

"That's silly," said Mary.

"We don't know," I said. "He might be a really cutthroat businessman with enemies."

Mary stared at me. "Seriously?"

"Hmm," Alex said, "how well do you know him?"

I pretended to notice something very interesting under the steps.

"Alex," Mary said, "I'm begging you, don't encourage her. She sees mysteries everywhere."

"I'm just curious," I mumbled.

"Yeah, the same curiosity got her in trouble in Virginia with her parents, the town, and the law," Mary said, stomping her foot.

"I was trying to save the fish. It ended up okay."

"Yes, and we're at an end right now. Even if your little 'Mr. Blanton's enemy' theory wasn't crazy, guests hardly ever come in through the back door. How could someone plan that?"

"Okay," I said, peeking through my bangs. "The target could be one of us."

"True," said Alex, laughing. "Or Ms. Gigi."

"Stop," said Mary. "Enough crazy talk."

I pointed at the nails resting in Alex's palm. "Okay, y'all might be right. But we won't save Ms. Gigi very much money by re-using those nails. Can we keep 'em just in case?"

Mary gave me an eye roll. "I'm not even going to ask 'in case of what?' But if it will make you happy, and let us all get back to work..."

I grinned, grabbed the nails, and thought, hah, my first piece of evidence.

Chapter 3

Around Every Corner

We spent a big chunk of the day touring the inn so I would know where to find cleaning supplies, towels, room items like tissues or sheets, trash bags and toilet paper for the bathrooms. I wrote stuff down in a little notebook my parents had given me. Mary thought that was a riot.

"Hey," I said, "when I found out I was coming here, I gave up that junior intern spot on our paper back home. But they said I could submit an article like 'My Summer in the Mountains' and they might run it. Hence, the notes. Plus, what if a guest asks me something simple, like do you have a spare toothbrush, and I don't know where one is?" I held up the notebook.

Mary nodded. "Maybe we should have waited until after eighth grade to take jobs."

"Ya think?" I said, giggling. "Too late now, we're in it." We'd pretty much finished going over things upstairs, and I pulled the inn's brochure from my back pocket. I opened it to the photos of the rooms. "Hey, where's this Whistle Creek one?"

Mary pointed toward the end of the hall and up. "There's technically a third floor, which is the attic. Our room is named for the teaberry plant and that one's named for the stream on the property. It's actually a second floor porch that was enclosed, and it's up like four steps, but not quite to the third floor. C'mon, we'll knock and peek in, but we have guests staying there, so they could be back any time." She reached in her pocket, fished out a lanyard attached to a set of keys, and handed it to me. "Gram said she hoped you liked blue and white."

I grinned. "Aw, UNC's colors. That's where my dad went." Hanging the lanyard around my neck like Mary, I suddenly felt very official. I followed her up the little set of stairs and watched her knock softly on the door of the Whistle Creek room.

After her knock, she said, "Housekeeping." When no one answered, she used her key.

I nodded, and wrote that in my notebook. It sounds stupid, but it's exactly the thing you want to remember so you don't interrupt a guest who is hopping out of the shower. (Awkward!)

Mary opened the door and we stood there a moment gazing at twin beds made of rustic cedar poles, dressed with hand-stitched quilts and matching pillows. Photos of area trout streams hung on the walls, and throw rugs with fishing poles woven into the design covered the floor. A bowl on the dresser held a collection of antique wooden whistles. Two comfy-looking chairs faced a TV on a small wooden cabinet. "Currently, the guests staying in here are two guys."

"Guys? They're very neat."

Mary nodded. "Yeah, they just don't bring much. They work for a fancy craft store here, but they don't live in Winton. They travel a lot for the company and stay here when they're in town. The owner of the store pays their tab, and he won't pay for two rooms, so they're both in here. It's complicated, but the store owner is one of Gram's friends, Evan Moss."

I shrugged. "Okay."

"Gram says business people love B&Bs because they get tired of life on the road and want something homier."

We started down the hall, and I sniffed the fresh cut lilacs in the pottery vase on a corner table. This was a neat place, and while not like my home, it *was* very homey. "Um, question. I'm hungry again, so what do I do?"

"Gram usually cooks for us at dinner, but we're on our own for lunch," said Mary. "Let's do a flash kitchen tour, and I'll show you where to find food and stuff for snacks. Gram made spaghetti sauce for tonight, and I'll get out the pasta pot while we're down there. Race ya."

Mary veered toward the back stairs and I sprinted down the front ones. At the bottom, I swung around the banister and all but crashed into two men standing in the lobby. I guess they'd heard me on the stairs, because they stepped back before I could mow them down. People popping up unexpectedly was a surprise I guess I'd get used to, but one minute you felt like this place was your home, and the next there were perfect strangers sticking their hand out to you.

"Hello, miss," said the taller one. He was skinny like a distance runner and was probably about my dad's age, but his lined face made me think he'd spent lots of time outdoors. Dressed in rumpled khakis, golf shirt, and scuffed-up boat shoes, this guy looked nice, but I would guess he didn't own one suit or tie.

"Hi," I said, shaking his hand, and wondering what to do next. "I'm Emily Sanders. Let me get Mary."

"Nah," said the other guy. He set down some Target bags and showed me a room key. He was much younger, dark-skinned with close-shaven dark wiry hair, and he was dressed in jeans, grey T-shirt, and black sneakers. "We're guests. No need to bother Miss Mary. I'm Jamal Greene, and he's Clayton Shaw. It's nice to meet you."

"Same here." I pointed to the bags. "Exciting afternoon in Winton, yes?"

Jamal laughed, and said, "New clothes. We just finished work, and the last couple days I got glue *and* paint on my shorts. It's hot where we're headed next trip, so I wanted to be comfortable on the road."

"Oh, you're with that shop Mary was telling me about," I said. "So you two make some of the crafts?"

"Us? That would be a no," Jamal said, glancing at Mr. Shaw. "It's just sometimes they need touching up or a little repackaging."

As they headed up the stairs, I stood thinking those bags looked way heavier than a couple pair of shorts. Then I then realized how snoopy that probably was, so I kept moving toward the kitchen. While my second guest encounter did not involve first aid, I'd almost knocked someone down. Getting better, but plenty of room for improvement.

When I burst into the kitchen, Mary spoke up from beside the massive fridge. "You won't win one race this summer if you can't do better than that."

"Hey, no worries. I was doing the whole greet-the-guest thing. I met the guys, and FYI, they're not traveling light this trip."

"Really? What do you mean?"

"Yeah, they were chitchatting about going to Target for some new shorts, but the stuff in the bags appeared to be lots heavier than that."

Mary squinted her eyes at me and whispered. "Em, does your crazy imagination ever shut off? Lots of people go shopping for one thing and come home with ten. You'll go crazy if you try to analyze every guest here this summer. Let it go."

I sighed. "Okay."

She gave me a thumbs-up. "However, you get a pass on the race, and points for making the guests come first."

Just then, Grandma Gigi came hustling down the back stairs into the kitchen. She stretched her arms and said, "Thanks for the nap time, girls. Did I just hear 'making the guests come first?'"

We nodded.

"That calls for a little reward." Gigi grabbed a marker and wrote *Girls off Monday night!* on the kitchen whiteboard. "Now, I need to check the inn's emails and get dinner going."

Mary said, "Sounds good, Gram. I'm showing Em the layout of the pantries, where to find supplies, food for lunch, stuff like that. Do you want me to put the spaghetti sauce on simmer?"

"Sure," said Gigi, over her shoulder. "Then take Emily for a quick bike ride on the trails. When you're done, put two fresh bikes in the front rack for the Randalls."

Mary handed me a banana and led me on a food tour of the kitchen and the three pantries. It was jam-packed, so it didn't seem possible we'd ever run out of anything. There was plenty of stuff to make grilled cheese sandwiches and lots of cans of soup, so I would not starve here. Mary hollered to Gram as we headed out, and then said, "Two things. Alex texted he'll be over later to fix the step. And bikes live in the carriage house. Come on, more notes to take."

I shook my head. Imagine, some kids get to laze around all summer playing video games. "Okay, Junior Boss, are you ever gonna stop with the instructions?"

"Yup," Mary answered with a grin. "I'll stop the moment my butt hits that bike seat. You're leading us on the trail, and we don't eat unless you find our way back."

Okay, I was still hungry, so blackmail was enough to get me to pay attention to putting air in the tires and adjusting the seats. Finally, we took off.

~

When we got to the edge of the woods, I stopped to check out the trail signs. There were two marked trails through the Baird's Den woods, open to hikers, bikers, and horses. That was neat except when you thought about skidding through horse poop, but hopefully we wouldn't have to deal with that today. With dinner looming, I chose the shorter trail and we took off following the blue signs. "Who put the signs up?" I yelled.

Mary called from behind me. "Alex and a buddy of his. I've never seen any horses back here, but lots of hikers, so be on the lookout. We have those trail bells on the handlebars or you can just call out—"

I hollered back, "I know, 'on the left.' We'll see the stream, yes?"

"Yup."

I glanced through the trees. The sun was still up, but the shadows got bigger the further into the woods we rode. I shivered, not exactly scared, just glad I wasn't alone for my first time in here. This trail was mostly downhill. Near the lowest part, I saw an L-shaped symbol, and the lower part of the L had a little drawing of waves. I signaled for a turn and soon we heard rushing water. We came to the creek itself way sooner than I expected and skidded parallel to it, following along the pebble-covered bank. After maybe a quarter of a mile we stopped to rest against a little log footbridge. "Aw, this is so cute. Do we have time to cross over and explore the other side?"

Mary swigged some water and shook her head. "Sorry, we don't. It's harder than you think going back because it's mostly uphill. We'd best move along." She glanced over my shoulder, and said, "Oh, hi."

I whipped around and saw a hiker coming from deeper in the forest. He tipped his baseball hat, adjusted his backpack, and strode on past us up the path. At the fork he got onto the red trail, which veered to the right; our trail went back to the left. I swallowed hard, reached over and swiped Mary's water. After a couple gulps, I handed it back to her and said, "A, Thanks. B, I'm normally not a fraidy cat. But, even though you warned me, I can't get used to people just popping up everywhere. In the house, and now in the woods. Gah!"

Mary shrugged. "You will. That guy's been by recently. Did you see his binoculars?"

Now that I could speak, I realized I had. "Yup, what do those mean?"

"He's a birder—they're all over the place up here. They spot birds, do research. Very intense, nice, but sometimes a little geeky."

"Okay, got it."

"Um," Mary said, "you doin' okay with everything?"

"No worries," I said, looking around. "Ready to head back? It's getting dark down here."

Mary nodded. "It is, but keep looking up. The sun's still out, but it gets shadowy back in here in the afternoon. Want me to lead?"

No way did I want to be the last one in the woods. "Oh, no. Remember, you said I had to find the way back. I love a challenge." Also, getting out alive. Besides the random hikers roaming around here, I was certain I didn't want to run into an "occasional" bear.

Chapter 4

Teamwork is Not Just for Football Players

Monday morning, I slipped into the kitchen through the back door to the sound of clinking utensils and the smell of fresh coffee brewing. Earlier, I had made the first pot before leaving for my run. I summoned up my public smile, stepped into the dining room, and nodded to our guests. "Good morning."

"Good morning, young lady," Mr. Randall said. "Miss Mary here has fixed us a fine breakfast. I understand you made this wonderful coffee. This all is just what we need to get going this morning. Kudos to everyone."

"Thank you," said Mary, filling the water glasses. "When it's ready, Em, could you grab that fresh pot?"

"Sure," I said, pointing to three empty chairs. "Anyone else up yet?"

Mary nodded. "The guys just grabbed coffee and biscuits to go."

"Right, I saw them out by the dumpster."

"Hope it wasn't the biscuits," said Mary, laughing. "Anyway, we probably won't see them until later on. I carried Mr. Blanton's breakfast up to him. He's doing great, just sore."

"Emily," said Mrs. Randall, "where do you run this early in the morning?"

"Oh, I was just exploring," I said. "I ran twelve minutes in one direction, and twelve minutes back. I have to stay in shape for swim team. Especially with all this good food."

"True," said Mr. Randall. "That's why we'll be hopping on those bikes again today."

I heard Mary cooing behind me as I headed back to the kitchen. "What a great idea! When Em gets back with coffee, she'll clear these plates. Sound good?"

I shut the door behind me, giggling at the sound of Mary schmoozing the guests. Then I turned around and stopped short, not believing the scene. Pots littered the stove. Flour was scattered across the slate gray tile floor like a snowfall. What a mess!

I heard the sound of feet on the back stairs, and Gigi peeked into the kitchen. "Is it safe to come in?"

"Only if you know how many pans it takes to cook breakfast for five people."

Gigi shook her head and pointed to the stove. "Well, evidently it's still taking a bunch."

I nodded. "Now I know why you asked me to help her with breakfast. It sure wasn't because I can cook, although the Randalls raved about my coffee."

"Fantastic! Leave the last of the first pot for me, and take them the fresh one. Think there's any food left?"

I laughed, and started a sinkful of soap and water. "I'm hoping sausage biscuits are in that bread basket and juice is in the fridge."

Gigi said, "I'll save you some of whatever I find. We still have some peaches, and I hear you like fruit. Just toss those pans in the sink to soak and Mary will scrub them. For you this morning, it'll just be a quick pass in the guys' room and the Randalls'. You'll make beds, give a wipe around the bathrooms, grab dirty towels, and leave stacks of fresh ones in each room. That's it. However, Mr. Blanton will be checking out soon, so later his will be a full clean."

"Okay," I said, "sounds like a plan." Inside I was thinking, eek, I'm supposed to do all that this *morning*?!

"But, right now, deliver that coffee, then eat," Gigi insisted. "I'm going to take mine out back and read the paper. We'll have our little meeting about eleven."

I dried my hands, tucked a tray under one arm, and grabbed the coffee pot. I stepped into dining room, did the pouring and clearing thing, then staggered back, thankful we only serve one meal a day.

Later, the three of us settled in around the kitchen island. "Well, Emily, you lived through your first twenty-four hours here."

I grinned. "And except for random people popping up, I haven't felt like running away yet."

They laughed, and Mary said, "That's good, because we want you to stay. The guests loved your coffee, and we're going to have some wild times here, like tonight."

"We?"

"Yeah," said Mary, "it's Cabbage Night."

I wrinkled my nose and looked at Gigi, who nudged me with her foot. "Trust us. It's pretty neat. Some people wait all year for it. Mary will explain."

I remembered my parents had been worried I would spin out of control up here with no supervision. Oh, my gosh, I forgot to call my parents! Wow, maybe that was a sign. Of what I wasn't sure, but things weren't horrible here. Okay, we were so busy, I could barely hold my head up and it wasn't even afternoon yet. But really, even after dark, how much trouble could I get into if our night on the town was something to do with a vegetable?

"All right, girls. Let's get serious. First, Em, do you have any questions or concerns?"

I frowned, then just plunged in. "I need to train for swim team, and part of it involves running. I went for a run this morning, then realized I probably should have cleared it with you first."

Gigi thought a minute. "Cleared it? Not really. You girls both need your workouts, but you probably should at least leave a note on the board in the kitchen. If you're on site, take a walkie-talkie with you. What else do you two need?"

Mary shrugged. "I would like uneven bars, but I at least need a balance beam. I was thinking maybe Alex could rig me one out of some scrap wood. And Em needs a pool."

I looked at them. "Speaking of pools, did either of you smell chlorine last night?"

Mary shook her head.

Gigi finished writing a note, and then looked at me. "Chlorine?"

I nodded. "Yeah, it was kind of strong. I woke up thinking I was in the pool locker room."

"Goodness, that's a puzzle. I went to bed so early, I can't really say if I smelled anything or not. Now, let me think about this workout stuff a bit. Thank you, Em, for not being too shy to ask me. But, what's this about encountering 'random people'?"

Mary interjected, "Oh, remember she met the craft shop guys on the stairs, and a few hours later we ran into the bird guy in the woods. I couldn't think of his name, so we just said 'hi'."

Gigi nodded. "We live in a kind of public place."

"I'm beginning to see that," I agreed.

"That fella's new with the Audubon Society," said Gigi, squinting like she was trying to remember something. "His name's... Jim Adams. I think he's doing research. Anyway, you'll quite likely see him around.

"Moving on. As you probably know, Jay Blanton came back last night, and he seems to be doing fine. Alex did a nice job on the step. My carpenter is working on the planter box." At the sound of the back door opening, she looked up from her notes. "Oops, here he is right now."

A short, stocky man wearing T-shirt, jeans, work boots, and leather tool apron stepped into the kitchen. Gigi smiled, and said, "Girls, this is Mr. Holton, and since my team left for China, I've been working him to death. Lyle, you remember my granddaughter, Mary. And this is Emily Sanders, our newest summer helper."

Mr. Holton tipped his hat, and said, "Hello, everyone. Gigi, I've finished repairing the planter box. I also checked the other steps, and tapped down a few nails, but other than that, they seem okay. It's still a bit of a mystery how those nails came all the way out, but as I said, all's well now."

"That's good to hear," said Gigi. "I appreciate you popping over on such short notice."

"Happy to help, ma'am."

I spoke up. "Mr. Holton, when Alex was here, we found some nails lying in the dirt. Could they have been the ones from the step?"

"I couldn't say, but I always police my work areas. I never leave nails in the dirt because they can be a hazard and it's not professional." He nodded to Ms. Gigi. "I'll just show myself out and finish up."

Gigi thanked him, and shut the door behind him. Then she poured more coffee, and sighed. "Lyle's one of the good guys. He suggested some safety-wise improvements that we should do before an inspector points them out."

"Safety? Like what?" asked Mary.

"Oh, attach railings to the porch, and add some fire extinguishers. He'll make nice wooden holders to match the inn's décor."

I nodded. "My mom would want that, very safe, but still charming."

"That does sounds like her," agreed Mary. "Okay, Gram, what's next? You wanted this to be a short meeting."

"I do, but Em looks like she's pooping out." Gigi reached over to the cookie jar, slid it toward me, and said, "Maybe you need a treat."

"Wow, I forgot about those." I hopped off the stool and grabbed a Baird's Den chocolate chip cookie. I sat there a second or two, chewing and thinking. "Hmm, Alex said to ask about the secret ingredient." I sniffed, and looked at Mary. "Is it cinnamon?"

She nodded. "Good guesser. Most people just sit and sigh, but don't think of it."

"I love cinnamon."

"Well, wait until you have the fried apples later this week," said Gigi. "The cinnamon *makes* 'em."

"Oh, I love fried apples, too. I'm not sure if it's the taste or the smell," I said. "My aunt and uncle have an apple orchard, and she uses cinnamon in her fried apples too. That smell is one of the best things to wake up to."

Gigi said, "Well, before too long, that's how you'll know you're here. We've got lavender around for sleeping, cinnamon for mood and digestion, and everyone remembers the teaberry tea. Smells make a home home."

"Sure seems like it," agreed Mary. "I got a text from Alex. His mom said a new batch of cinnamon bears is ready."

"Really?" I asked. "Are they yummy?"

"You'd think so, being they're made from cinnamon and apple-sauce, but you don't eat them," Mary said, reaching into a cabinet. She pulled out a chubby, three-inch tall reddish-brown bear and sat him in my palm. "Smell."

I got a whiff and grinned. "Mmm! What are they for?"

"We give them as souvenirs of a stay at Baird's Den. With bears and all, these little statues are a play on Gram's last name, Baird. Alex's mom makes them just for us."

"How cute," I said, tapping the bear's head. "Do I hand them out?"

"No," said Gigi, "we keep them in the office supply closet. One per room, at checkout. Of course, that little guy can be yours."

"Aw, I'll name him after my brother," I said, "and hope this is as close as I get to a bear the whole summer."

~

When dinner was over, Mary said, "Okay, we're off duty."

"Almost," I said. "The carpenter said all the *other* nails were in good shape. It was just the nails on that particular step that came loose and it was a bit of a mystery. *See?*"

Mary sighed, and said, "Nice try. It's also the bottom step. That's the one everybody hits first. More wear and tear equals worn out wood and stress on the nails. So we're done with that. We're headed downtown for Cabbage Night."

I had noticed Mary had on pale green shorts with matching long sleeved T-shirt, and she was knotting a purple-trimmed-in-green scarf around her neck. "Okay, so you weren't kidding?"

"Cabbage is a big deal here. Farmers grow tons of it. I heard they used to have a factory that made sauerkraut. Cabbage is part of their history, like furniture and sweatshirts are part of ours. That's why one night is set aside for it during the Heritage Festival. Tonight, downtown is really busy, and it should be fun."

Neither of us spoke as we walked along, listening to the crickets and watching fireflies flit through the fir trees. Fir needles crunched under our feet, so it smelled like Christmas instead of early summer. As we neared Front Street, we were no longer alone. It seemed like the whole county had come to town. Cabbage Night had sounded stupid, but kids cheered on their entries in the Cabbage Derby, and folks in bib overalls hoisted their hefty orbs onto the scales hoping to win blue ribbons for the mightiest cabbage. Down the way a bit, amateur cooks passed out ballots for the "Cabbage Cuisine" contest. Who knew you could make a burger out of cabbage?

Arriving at the town square, we wove through the milling crowd and then wandered into Books and Stuff. Mary headed toward the art books, and I stopped to check out the fancy pens, journals and writing paper. Finally, we met at the door, sampling the snacks arrayed on tables, compliments of the merchants. When we got outside, I sipped some juice and asked, "Want to go to the tennis and golf shop?"

"If you need to we can," replied Mary. "Or the craft shop?" She pointed around a clown, who was juggling purple and green cabbages, to the checkerboard sign announcing "Mountain Artisans." She nudged me. "Come on."

As we got to the shop, I stopped at the front display windows. "Wow, look at this stuff." The first window was filled with handmade split oak baskets, grapevine wreaths and pillows in so many colors they looked like a rainbow. "Check out the quilts." Some were hung like art, others draped over ladder-back chairs. More filled wooden quilt racks.

"Mariella Ortiz, Alex's mom, made most of these. See, they've all got those red heart-shaped tags. So cute."

I scooted closer to the entrance. It gave me a view into the store, and there near the front counter stood a dark-haired man, dressed in a seafoam fishing shirt, shorts and boat shoes.

"That's the owner, Evan Moss," Mary said, tipping her head. "He's the one who sent us the Whistle Creek guys as guests."

"For an older guy, isn't he gorgeous?" asked a female voice behind us.

I said, "Excuse me?"

"Hi, Mel," said Mary. "Emily Sanders, meet Melanie Williams. She and her mom live around the corner from Gram."

I turned to find a girl who might have been our age, but looked like a Texas rodeo queen. Her long blonde hair was really poufy, and her makeup was pretty, but thick, as if she'd planned on being onstage tonight. She wore expensive-looking leather cowgirl boots, jeans and a black, long-sleeved button-down shirt. Melanie nodded, sending a little cloud of perfume my way. "Hey, welcome to Winton. So you're one of those Virginia girls, too?"

"Yup. But, my daddy's a Tar Heel."

"Oh, good, then you can stay!" said Melanie, giggling. "Townspeople are always curious about strangers. They always ask me stuff."

"Sure," I said, thinking, A, Did she just give me permission to stay? and B, Who says "townspeople"? I decided to play nice and be polite. "So, this Evan Moss guy has a great store."

"He's the best! He bought his condo from my mom's company. Now he's interested in another one."

"Melanie's mom is a realtor," said Mary. "What would he do with two condos?"

"I don't know, maybe live in one and rent the other. He's also hinting about buying investment property and/or somewhere to expand this place. Is Ms. Gigi ready to retire?"

Mary wrinkled her nose. "Are you kidding? She *loves* having Baird's Den."

"That's okay. Mom suggested he look at the Reynolds' house. It has lots of possibilities."

Mary gave her a long look. "Gol, Mel. Are you studying for your realtor's license?"

Melanie giggled. "Sorry, I just get wound up." She nudged me. "Hey, do you know that other man?"

Honestly, I hate being nudged by people I barely know, and I wished this pushy girl would run along. But there was something familiar about the tall guy standing by the credit card machine. He tapped a clipboard with a pen and turned toward the door. It was then I saw the binoculars. However, I decided on the spot to share no information whatsoever with the junior town crier. "*I* don't know him."

We watched as he came out of the store, tipped his hat at us, and disappeared into the crowd. "It might be our birder," said Mary. "He had sunglasses on when *we* saw him."

Melanie shrugged. "No biggie, I'd just never seen him before. Alex Ortiz's mom is there, too. I wondered if that guy was her boyfriend."

"Boyfriend?" I asked.

"Yeah," said Mary, nodding. "It's sad, but Alex's dad died of cancer a few years ago. She's really young to be a widow."

I sighed, not knowing what to say.

"Enough gloom," said Mary, stomping one of her hand-painted-to-match-the-outfit green sandals. "Come on, Em, I want you to meet her. Going in with us, Mel?"

"Not tonight, I'm going to input some of my mom's new listings in MLS." She nudged Mary. "Don't say a word, but my mom isn't very good on the computer."

Mary nodded and opened the shop door. "Next time we see you, you'll have a briefcase and business cards."

Melanie giggled again, then turned on the heel of her boots and headed off down the sidewalk. "See ya later."

I smiled one of those half, not real smiles. I heard a man's voice coming from inside the shop. "Mary Carnell, I am glad to see you. And I hope your friend is right behind you. I've got some new products for you two to work some magic on."

Mary waved to Mr. Moss and Alex's mom, and then turned to face me. "Um, I might have forgotten to mention, we sort of work for him, too."

I leaned my head toward Mary and whispered, "Work? As in a second job?"

She squeezed my arm, and nodded. "It's really fun, you'll love it, but right now, just remember more coins to buy your phone, and did I mention we'll have fun?!"

Chapter 5

Information Overload

We'd barely gotten in the door of Mountain Artisans when Mary's phone beeped with a text from Gigi. While she read it, I chatted with Alex's mom, who was in her late thirties, slender, and absolutely beautiful. Her chin length black hair was just as shiny as her son's, and she was friendly but not gushy. Mr. Moss had to speak to some customers, so I wandered around the shop tinkling the wind chimes and sniffing all sorts of balsam pillows and floral arrangements that were fake, but somehow smelled real. I never got to the soaps, lotions or candles, but with names like Lemon Pie, Very Vanilla, and Rippling Raspberry, the smells coming from them were scrumptious.

When Mary finished reading about the B & B inspector's "surprise" visit tomorrow, we decided to head back to the inn. Ms. Ortiz said she'd have Alex deliver the order of cinnamon bears in the next few days, and Mr. Moss assured us he'd contact Gigi to hear how things went.

Thankfully, I was used to life in a small town, or I'd think everybody was in somebody else's business up here.

On the way home Mary broke it down for me. Gram would be on site to answer questions or find documents like insurance papers, and her carpenter would tour the inspector around the property. After breakfast, Mary would do some office stuff, and I could take off. Gigi had come bustling up to me before we left for town. "I forgot to tell you my Y membership is still in force. And it can be expanded to guests and staff just by renewing for two years!"

"Is that a lot of money?"

"Oh, my goodness, it's not! Their pool is terrific, and our guests will love the perk, plus I can deduct it as a business expense. I'm so glad you asked me about it. Here's a copy of my card, just stop by the desk and they'll issue you a day pass."

"Cool, thanks! You can put that info in your brochure."

"Oh, I will in the next printing, and tomorrow, Mary can add it to my website."

~

The next morning, Gigi sent me off to the Y because, she said, the inspectors don't like seeing a lot of staff "hovering." They take it as the owners trying to distract them and cover stuff up. So, map in hand, I biked to town on my own. It was only a little over a mile, and pretty easy except for the sort of odd traffic. There were so many tourists here, and apparently none of them looked out their car windows. They missed a lot of amazing scenery peering at their GPSs and then made a lot of U-turns. Thankfully, that and not knowing where they were going made them drive super slowly. I sped right past them, thinking that here two wheels were way better than four.

The staffers at the Y processed the day pass really fast, gave me a tour, and handed me a towel. They said if I hurried, I'd beat the mob of kiddie campers who were due in from playing flag football, so I shoved my stuff in a locker and headed for the pool.

The pool itself was indoors, with one wall made of glass, which provided a neat view of the mountains. The opposite wall was made from giant garage doors, which were all raised today. Just outside were beach volleyball courts and a playground. Ropes for three lanes lined the pool, which was just perfect for the six of us doing laps. Two junior swimmers tried to pass me, one on each side. I remembered being just as annoying at that age, so I just cranked up my speed for a few minutes. Flipping over to backstroke, I grinned at them and waved as the distance between us grew wide.

Since no one said how long to stay away from the inn, I just winged it. I finished my laps and did some upper body work in the weight room. A boy showed me a cool thing with a medicine ball, and then asked where I was staying. I'm tall for my age, and sometimes people think I'm older than I am. This boy was probably in college, so I just replied something vague, like "with friends," and headed for the vending machine to grab a Payday candy bar to munch on the ride back. Still, he was cute! Pretty cool morning for me, no cleaning of any sort, *and* I got to swim. The only thing left to do was start on that surprise second job, but that might have to wait.

I rode up the driveway and saw the inspector standing on the front steps with his arm extended toward Gigi. He shook a wad of papers at her, and finally she pulled them from his hand. They didn't look like they'd become best friends while I was gone.

I saw Mary burst through the back door, and we met at the carriage house. "So, he's done?"

"Finally," Mary said, handing me the tire pressure gauge. We were supposed to check the air before and after using the bikes. "Yeah, first he seemed like he would zip through here and be on his way. But I think he opened every door in the inn, examined each step twice, shook railings and banisters, and the last thing I saw he was checking the temperatures in the freezers."

I finished with the bike and put it away. "Hey, you told me one night you were worried about killing someone with spoiled food."

Mary sighed. "True, so the freezer thing was probably a good idea. Otherwise, that report looked massive. Help me cut some lavender, and then we'll see what's up." She led the way to the garden.

I grabbed my backpack, and said, "Listen, the Y's neat. The gymnastics stuff for you looked great. I loved the pool. It seemed like forever since I did laps." As we neared the garden, I ducked and yelled, "Holy, bees!"

Mary grinned. "I know. They freaked me out the first time I came here in the summer. So much is blooming, we've got to share with nature."

I nodded, looking closely at the garden for the first time. She was right, plants and flowers were almost popping open right before our eyes. "Lots of pollination going on."

Mary shook her head. "You always act like you hate science, and then you shock me with some true comment like that."

"Some kid in my science class this year did a great report on bees. I remember his PowerPoint had images of a garden like this and how it was a big deal for the food chain." I shrugged. "What can I say, I love to eat. Go bees!"

"Good thing you think like that, cuz you'll see lots of them, and bunches of hummingbirds. Just shoo them away if you need to cut something."

"Okay," I said, "but y'all might need to label these things. I know what petunias look like, but past that, I can't tell an aster from a peony."

Mary tapped me on the head with the scissors, and then bent over to cut the lavender. When we came in through the kitchen, we saw Gigi on the phone, waving a wad of papers in front of her. "Even fire extinguishers, carbon monoxide monitors, additional smoke detectors, bracing on every railing inside and out, escape ladders for all the upper story rooms, and that's only page one, Evan!"

Mary turned to me and whispered, "This is good. She's talking to Mr. Moss. He usually can calm her down."

Gigi snapped her fingers at us and pointed to the bar stools at the island. I sat down, and Mary grabbed a pitcher of lemonade. Apparently it was okay that we listened, so we prepared to sit awhile. Mr. Holton came in the back door.

Gigi held her hand over the phone, and said, "Lyle, just have a seat with the girls and I'll be right with you." She turned her attention back to the phone. "Goodness, that's nice of you. I'll think about it, and call you back. Thanks for your help." She clicked the phone off. "Lyle, wasn't that some crazy morning?"

He slid his baseball cap back and scratched his head. "Yes, ma'am, one for the books. But in the long run it could save you some big headaches."

Gigi smiled and shook her head. "You're ruining my perfectly good tantrum! Okay, I'll stop whining and put my business owner's hat on. What's the estimate on the work?"

He pushed a legal pad toward her. "I'll email you a printed copy, but this will take care of the required items in the report. The rest of that stuff is 'suggested,' so we'll deal with that later on. My estimate is only for the page one items. The attic work probably should be done by someone with more electrical experience."

Gigi grabbed her cell phone and started adding up numbers. She sighed. "The total is staggering, but the work's necessary. I'll write you a check, but please don't cash it for a day or so. To cover all this, I'll need to access the line of credit at the bank. With a new furnace system this spring, the medical bills after my fall and the ambulance for Mr. Blanton, whew!" She motioned for Mary to pour some lemonade for Mr. Holton. "I wasn't happy with the inspector's comment about the toilet aroma outside. Early this spring we spread manure in the garden. Could that be it?"

"I don't know, ma'am. My sniffer doesn't work all that well anymore. The septic system here has some age on it. Have you had any issues lately with the toilets?

"Girls?" asked Gigi.

We looked at each other and tried not to giggle. Mary said, "This morning we thought someone had passed a massive amount of gas."

I nodded. "Then we realized the smell was coming in through the window."

Mr. Holton cleared his throat. "It might not be a bad idea if Pete checked it out. You don't want sewage problems with an inn full of guests."

Gigi sighed. "It never ends! Listen, even with all the repairs, I don't want to look like we're under construction. If possible, let's work during the middle of the day. Guests check out by 11:00 and don't arrive until after 3:00. Girls, we need every reservation we've got, and somehow we have to figure how to get more."

Mary asked, "What did Mr. Moss say?"

Gigi nodded. "Oh, right. One of his guys, Clayton, the tall one, has lots of electrical experience and does some of his repairs at different properties. Evan said he'd donate Clayton's time and we could take it off the bill for the room charges when the guys stay here. So, he could take care of the attic work and the smoke detectors."

"Wow," I said, "that's pretty generous."

Mr. Holton nodded. "Yup, it is, and it might just do the trick. If you sign off on this, I'll have supplies here by tomorrow, Ms. Gigi."

"Sounds good. Just tell them to call with the total, and I'll give them a credit card over the phone. I'm pretty sure I've got one that's not maxed out yet," she said, zipping her pen across the clipboard. "I'll walk you out and snip a few roses for the tables."

As we watched them leave, I looked at Mary, and said, "Don't yell."

She squinted. "Why would I?"

I said, "Is it like common knowledge that Gigi's having hard times financially?"

Mary shrugged. "I'm not sure, but lots of people up here are having problems. Apparently, the last two ski seasons were a bust because they didn't get much snow. There used to be tons of antique shops, and now there are only two. The hobby shop just closed, but the bakery and hardware store are still doing okay. Mr. Moss is too. But Gram thinks that's because he ships so much out of town, and doesn't just rely on just the local foot traffic or the tourists who wander in looking for a souvenir. She also says if you believe the realtors, they're not doing well either, but that doesn't stop them from pestering her to sell."

"Like Melanie last night."

Mary nodded. "Yeah, Gigi will never do it, but investors want this property to fill the woods with condos and turn the inn itself into a clubhouse or conference center."

"Ick," I said, and pointed to Mary. "See? Maybe the step was *not* an accident."

"Okay," said Mary, shaking her head. "Now I might yell."

"Yeah, I know. Hopefully, no one would be that mean to your gram. Forget I mentioned it."

Later, Mary called the Y. The fitness director was in, so she went up to look around. Gigi was thinking about gathering some teaberry leaves when we heard a vehicle coming onto the property. She peeked out the office window and said, "Oh, I had no idea he'd get by here today. Em, please motion him to go around back."

I sprinted out the front door and waved at the tanker-style truck to keep going. The *Pete's Plumbing* driver nodded and pulled in behind the back deck. The truck itself was quite spiffy, shiny even, but it still was icky to think about what might be inside the tank. Lettering on the truck read "Nobody Sticks Thar Nose in Our Business" so I guess Mr. Pete had a sense of humor about his work. Ms. Gigi came out to talk to him, and I went back in to gather up the trash from the entire inn.

I assembled several bagfuls, and resolved that after this summer, I'd never complain to my mom again about emptying the trash at home. No matter how green we tried to be, Baird's Den accumulated massive amounts of junk, garbage and debris. Pick a word, it was still trash, and I headed toward the dumpster with my haul. I looked out toward the garden and saw the plumber putting a big round metal plate back in the ground. He turned it with a long metal crowbar-shaped thing, like he was turning a screwdriver. I flung the trash bags into the dumpster and firmly shut the gates. As I headed back toward the inn, Mr. Pete looked at Gigi who stood a ways away from him in the grass.

"Well, at this juncture, I don't see anything mechanical to be at fault. So, that makes me think the bacteria in the tank may have been compromised in some way."

"Compromised?"

"Yes, ma'am, all but dead," he said, shoving his hands in the pockets of his coveralls. "You know bacteria are what make a septic system work, and if they die off, things start going south in a hurry."

"Is there anything we might have done to kill them?" asked Gigi. "We have several new people on staff this summer."

He shrugged. "Well, if your yard guy dumps oil down a toilet, that's not good. Or pesticides. Let's see, sometimes people get crazy trying to get rid of stains, and use way too much bleach. You've got a commercial washing machine, so figuring out how much detergent and bleach for big loads can be tricky."

Oh, no. Could I have accidentally caused this huge catastrophe for the inn? I gulped that thought down, and focused back on what Pete was saying.

"Cigarette butts and baby wipes are pretty bad for a system, too. Any of those things could be what happened here, though I don't find a blockage otherwise. Or, it could be the tank is wearing out, as it looks pretty old. I suggest we try an additive for a couple days. If that gets those bacteria rejuvenated, that's great. If not, we'll have to pump the tank and recharge it with bacteria."

As I neared the kitchen door, I peeked back over my shoulder. Gigi shuddered and waved me into the house. "Goodness gracious, we don't want that, so let's hope your first idea works."

"Well, either way, I'll leave a copy of my report. If the smell hasn't disappeared by the next time the inspector comes, you can show him you took some action. That should keep him from reporting you to the health department. I'll be back in a few days to retest. No need to pay me until we get a final total."

Wow, poor Gigi. Things just kept piling up for her. I glanced at all the gorgeous flowers planted and brilliant green grass that carpeted the area above the dreaded tank. Who knew something full of sludge lurked under all that pretty? I'd started a "stuff I learned this summer" list, and in my head I added, "You never know what the ground is hiding."

Chapter 6

What's Up?

A little while before dinner, I was lazing out on one of the porch swings staring at crafts from Mountain Artisans when I heard a *thump, thump*. Alex came up the driveway, carrying a box under one arm and bouncing a basketball with the other. I hit "Save" on my laptop. "Do you go all over town like that?"

"Sometimes."

I waggled my fingers. "Bet it helps make your hands stronger and gives you practice dribbling around obstacles."

He nodded. "It does, plus I'm breaking in a new ball."

I reached out and he passed it to me. I rolled it around in my hands and bounced it a couple times. "Feels like a good one."

"It's way better than any I've had before. It was a gift from Mr. Moss."

"Nice."

"Yeah, it was. Mom told him how she'd accidentally crushed my old one backing out of the driveway. He felt sorry for me because I was practicing with a beach ball."

I laughed. "You're kidding."

"Yeah, a little." He grinned and sped up his dribble. "Skills, missy, skills. . ."

"Where do you play?"

Alex said, "I'm in the Y league now, and hope to make JV at school."

"That's cool," I said. "Um, Mary told me about your dad dying. I'm really sorry."

"Thanks," replied Alex. "He coached some of my teams, like Little League. No matter what sport I was playing, he never missed a game. I'll be pumped if I get on JV as a freshman, but it would be even better if he could see me."

He was so serious for a guy, but this explained it perfectly. He was also really cute, but probably played guard, because, seriously, he was not super tall. I sighed for both of us.

"Yeah, that's got to be tough," I said. "Maybe your dad's watching over you."

He smiled. "That's what my mom keeps saying."

"Hey, I met her, and she seems to know her stuff!"

"Speaking of her," he said, lifting the box he'd been carrying. "I've got bears for the inn." He handed the box to me and pointed to the table. "What are you doing?"

I gave him a look. "I'm trying to describe this stuff. Come up with some amazing words, and I'll get you some water." I clapped my hands like "chop-chop" and headed for the kitchen.

He wrinkled his nose. "I'll take water, but no promise of anything amazing. Remember, I'm the lawn guy."

I returned and handed him a glass of water "Here's the deal. Mary and I were hired to create hangtags for this stuff. Mr. Moss loaded us up with two bags crammed full of items from the shop. Mary does the artwork." I held up some of her pencil sketches.

Alex took them from me and studied them for a few moments. "These are amazing. She should be in a gallery." Then he blushed. "Er, not her of course. Her work, like these."

I grinned. Aw, he liked my buddy. This was awesome, or it might be if she felt the same way about him. "Yeah, I know. She's won prizes for her art. Anyway, I do the writing. No prizes here, and I need *words* to describe it all." I switched to a fake announcer voice. "Pillows that smell like pine forests, fragrant florals that look just picked, and charming hand-painted baskets. Memories of the mountains with the 'Artisan' touch!"

"Yeah, that!" said Alex. "Those are good words."

"You big chicken," I said, laughing.

Just then, Gigi pushed open the screen door and said, "Hi, Alex. Did I hear you're afraid of something?"

I nodded. "Yes, ma'am, I need some clever words, and he says he doesn't have any. I'd heard he was good at everything."

Gigi nodded. "Well, he is, so don't be too hard on him. Lyle Holton was just saying earlier what a nice job he did on repairing the step."

Alex elbowed me, and said, "See? Hands not head!"

Gigi laughed. "Best thing I've heard all day."

"Ms. Gigi," I asked, "did Mr. Holton ever say anything more about why the nails popped out?"

"Nope," she said, "but we were pretty busy with the inspector. It was probably the farthest thing from his mind."

I looked at Alex and shrugged. I didn't care what he and Mary said. That step was not far from my mind, but right now I needed to figure out what to say about a watermelon-scented candle.

~

At dinner, Gigi told us about the plumber's visit, and we filled Gigi in on our afternoon. Mary sounded really jazzed about the gymnastic equipment at the Y and I pled my case for a definite mystery about the nails. Gigi agreed it did sound odd. I don't think she thought it was super-important, but she said we could be on the lookout for anyone suspicious. It sounded kind of stupid, even to me, as everyone around here was someone we knew. Okay, except for one person.

We were sitting next to each other, so I nudged Mary with my foot. "Hey, that bird guy makes it to the top of my suspect list."

She shook her head. "You are certifiable."

"Oh, please, little kids are taught to recognize that 'uh-oh' feeling about people," I said, "and he, for sure, gives me that feeling."

As Mary rolled her eyes, Gram laughed at both of us. "Did Emily tell you Alex stopped by?"

Mary shook her head. "Nope, nobody mentioned it to me. What did he want?"

"I wasn't really sure," I said. "He was on foot, dribbling a basketball that was a gift from Mr. Moss."

"Really?" asked Mary. "Maybe he came by to show it to me."

"Could be, it was a nice one," I said. "But he actually was delivering cinnamon bears. They're in the office."

After dinner, we arranged the crafts in the dining room, then brainstormed art and words. Ms. Ortiz's tags were already adorable with the heart on brown cardstock, so for the new items I wanted to be up to her standards. We're not advertising wizards, so the other crafts were hard to label at first. Then, we talked about why people buy this stuff and what they do with it. When we did that, ideas spewed forth. Before long, we printed drafts of some pretty decent hangtags. This actually wasn't such a bad job.

Gigi showed Jamal and Mr. Shaw how to access the attic, and they located spots for the smoke detectors. They stashed a ladder in the upper hall closet to be ready when the supplies arrived tomorrow. She said they'd check out right after they finished tomorrow night. The guys seemed nice, though they weren't too chatty. Honestly, that was great, because sometimes we had to talk to people way too much for me. As we packed up the crafts to take them to the shop the next day, I said, "Those guys are very different."

Mary nodded. "If you mean Jamal Greene is younger, black, short and muscular, and Clayton Shaw is older, white, tall and skinny, I agree. Oh, yeah, Jamal is married and Mr. Shaw is not."

"Wow, they must be here a lot if you know all that."

"About twice a month, I think. And whenever they come, they drive a different vehicle."

I shrugged. "Wow, that's awesome."

"I guess," said Mary. "They must like driving cuz every time they leave, they're headed somewhere different making deliveries."

"Of *crafts*?" I asked.

Mary stuffed a few more pillows in one of the shopping bags. "Apparently this stuff is popular everywhere. Alex said his mom had to hire a few more mountain ladies because she can't keep up."

"That's wild," I said. "Too bad I'm not crafty. You could sign me up for a third job."

Mary threw a pillow at me and I chased her around the lower level until we heard Grandma Gigi clear her throat and say in a surprisingly stern voice, "Girls?"

We peeked around the banister, where we saw her pointing at the wall clock.

I said, "My fault, Ms. Gigi. We misplaced the cookies."

Gigi covered a smile with her hand, and shook her head. "Nice try."

"Would you like some teaberry tea, Gram?"

"It would be great, but I'm so tired I don't want to wait for it to steep. Maybe just some warm milk with a cinnamon stick, and if you locate the cookies, I'll have one."

"Yes, ma'am," I said, and we hightailed it to the kitchen for the sweetest time of day. We only had five guests in total, one couple, a businesswoman meeting with the chamber of commerce, and the two guys. So including Gigi, we only had to fix four trays, and we had this down to a mini-assembly line. We did the first two and I ran them upstairs so Gigi's milk wouldn't get cold. The only kind of milk I like warm is hot chocolate, so I wouldn't consider this a treat.

I tapped on Gigi's door, and she called me in. She was curled up in a lounge chair, and she looked worn out. "Thanks for bringing this up, Em. One thing—remember downstairs is a quiet zone after 8:30."

"Yes, ma'am," I said, setting a napkin and cookie on the side table.

"Best remind my granddaughter, too," Gigi said. She pointed to the mug. "This really hits the spot, and the cinnamon stick in it is perfection."

I smiled and gently pulled the door shut. When I got back downstairs, Mary was on the phone, smiling and placing cookies on the other trays.

"Wow, Melanie, that sounds fun. I'd be happy to after we work out." She listened as the caller undoubtedly giggled her way through the phone call.

"Sure, I'll ask Gram if she needs any other summer help. I'm not sure about putting one of those real estate brochure holders here at the inn. She might be interested, so I'll try and get you in the door. See ya tomorrow." Mary hung up and whirled around looking sort of guilty.

"Are these ready?" I asked, pointing to the trays.

"You heard, I guess."

"Realtor girl is looking for a job?"

"Yeah, she wondered about offering walking tours. Gram usually likes to do them, but she probably won't be able to until the fall. I'll mention it."

"You'd be good at that."

"Thanks, but it'd be better with a local."

"Right," I said, "and besides, your hair isn't poufy enough."

"Hush," Mary said, pouring lemonade. "She's not so bad."

"Yeah, maybe." I glanced at my stubby fingernails, cut-off jean shorts and T-shirt smudged with gunk from my day job. "I just always feel dorky around people with manicures and fancy clothes."

Mary squinted. "You shouldn't, because that's not who you are. Anyway, her mom's redoing the logo for the agency, and wants my input. Their yoga teacher's doing a home visit tomorrow. So I'm invited for yoga, a healthy snack, and to see the art samples."

I love yoga and tried not to look jealous. "Wow, sounds fancy. Make sure everything you wear matches!"

Mary shook her head. "You're a riot." She glanced around. "Is that someone at the front door?"

I peeked up the hall and saw Moss's guys. Jamal Greene held up an extension cord.

Mary appeared beside me with the trays, and Mr. Shaw said, "If one of those is ours, I'll take it. Save y'all a trip."

Mary happily handed off the tray to Mr. Shaw, and carried the other one upstairs to the business lady. I grabbed my own cookie and milk and wolfed it down as I ran up to our room. I paced while I waited for my dad's old laptop to connect to Skype. Soon, I was waving at Mom wondering how she would start off. My mom could be such a drama queen.

"Oh, you *are* alive! We figured if something terrible had happened to you, the inn would eventually notify us."

I grinned. "Mom, it's only been three days. And, you know I'm working, right?"

"So funny. And you know, to us, it feels like you've been gone three months. How is it? Are you getting enough to eat?"

"We start the day with a humongous, fancy breakfast and end it with homemade chocolate chip cookies."

"Sounds like a 'yes' to me. Are the people nice?"

"The guests are very nice but you never know when you'll run into one, so you can't be like picking your nose or anything."

"On the job training," said Mom laughing. "I bet Mary's glad you're there."

"I think so. I found out she's not too great with blood. A guest fell and cut his head so I had to administer first aid."

"Is he going to be okay?"

"Yes, he checked out and went back to work Monday."

"I'm proud of you being able to help. Does that sort of thing happen often?"

"No, it's pretty unusual," I said. "Let's see what else? We've been out on the town one night."

"By yourselves, after dark?"

"Mom, we went downtown to Cabbage Night, which believe it or not is part of the Heritage Festival here. Not too much crazy happens except the Mightiest Cabbage weigh-in competition was pretty intense. Hey, is Ben still up?"

"Aw, honey. He's actually over at Granny J's having a sleepover."

I smiled, picturing him with his tiny duffle bag and stuffed Pooh Bear. "Rats, I wanted to read him a bedtime story."

"Try him later in the week. She's got a whole activity list for him."

"That sounds like Granny J." I spun the computer around to show Mom our room and the closet.

"Wow, you actually make your bed up there in the mountains. Now, I know there's more. Spill it."

"Mom, A, it's different than I expected, and B, it's not horrible."

"There's the positive-sounding kid I know and love."

"You're a riot. There's a lot of stuff to get used to, but I'm kind of figuring it out as I go."

"Cool beans, sugar. But, if you get stuck for an answer . . ."

I nodded, and knew if I didn't hang up I'd start blubbering. "I'll email or Skype again soon. Hug Dad and Ben. Love you." And I signed off.

There was a knock on the door, and Mary said, "I need to pick my clothes out for tomorrow. Okay, to come in?"

I said, "Sure." Hmm, back home seemed to be functioning perfectly fine without me. My friend here seemed happy making plans without me. That hurt a little, but I was pretty sure Gigi needed me so, for now, I planned to stick it out.

Chapter 7

Not Again!

Wednesday was crazy after Mary cleaned up from breakfast and left for her yoga event. I wasn't sure if there was a theme involved, but Mary looked very ethereal as she rode away wearing pale lilac leggings, a lilac and white zebra pattern long-sleeved tunic, matching head band, and white flip-flops. Then Alex arrived to mow, a truck from the hardware store delivered supplies for the repairs, and Grandma Gigi went to the bank. Somehow, the cleaning girl, a.k.a. me, got left in charge!

First, I assured the businesswoman that the faint sewer smell wafting up from some of the commodes was addressed late yesterday and should be fine by the end of day today. Next, I was returning from starting a load of towels when Alex popped in the back door. "Hey! If you're done mowing, I could use some help."

He gave me a look, shook his head, and said, "You don't want me in here for long. Sweat pouring off me, and all that."

I sniffed, but even though he wasn't stinky, he was pretty drippy. "Yeah, I see that now." I tossed him an old kitchen towel, and said, "Feel free to get some water. I've got to grab the phone." It was Gigi saying she would be home soon and asking me to keep holding down the fort, and that if Alex wanted to wait, she had money for him. I told him.

"Sure, I'll wait," he said, reaching into his back pocket. "You'll have to let these dry out, but I brought some passes for Magic Mountain."

I grinned so big. "You're kidding. Those are expensive, yes?"

Alex shrugged, and said, "Sure, if you're not connected."

"Like the mafia?"

"More like a volunteer. I needed service hours for school so now I'm one of the park's train troopers. Sort of a goofy name, but we *do* get to work on the trains."

"Even like Little Toot?"

He nodded. "It's pretty cool. I get to do that and take kids on tours of the engines."

"Aw, I love that place. My parents used to take me there when I was younger. Mom might bring Ben to the mountains later in the summer, and we'll all go."

Just then, Gigi came bustling in the door. "I heard that! Where will we all go?"

Good thing I wasn't keeping a secret from anyone. I kept forgetting voices travel easily through the old vents of the public rooms. "To Magic Mountain. Alex brought some passes."

"Oh, that's wonderful," said Gigi. "What are the chances of a behind-the-scenes tour?"

Alex smiled. "I can make that happen, Ms. Gigi."

I said, "I was telling him Ben might come ride the train this year."

Gigi nodded. "Perfect! We'll close down for the afternoon, and make it an employee event, Ben and your mom included!"

Alex glanced toward the clock. "I didn't see Mary around, so will you tell her I left a pass for her, too?"

"For sure, we'll let Mary know about the big plans." Gigi rummaged in her wallet and pulled out some cash. "Hah! I remembered to get this while I was at the bank." She sighed. "Dealing with bankers wears me out, but I need to get some things done in the office. Em, you are off the clock for a few hours. So, begone! And as far as I'm concerned, you and Mary can skedaddle from here again tonight. Evan's guys will be working in the attic, and we have no other guests until tomorrow."

"Sounds good," I said. "Right now, I'm gonna shoot up to the Y for some laps."

Alex headed out the back door, and said, "I've got a game at 7:30 up there if you two want to come."

"We might," I said, "I'll check with yoga girl."

~

We had soup and salads for dinner in the kitchen, and soon wished we'd chosen somewhere quieter. Mr. Shaw and Jamal decided the back stairs would be the shortest way to the attic, so they parked their vehicle behind the inn. They made a bunch of trips toting the wire, smoke detectors, and tools. Jamal just had a tool belt, but Mr. Shaw had a toolbox the size of a suitcase. I eyed it and he grinned. "Grew up on a farm where we always had tools. I'm ready for anything with this baby!"

I laughed and said, "Wow, my dad would be so jealous. His is more like a little tackle box."

They finally seemed to get everything they needed, and Mary finished telling us about her big yoga experience. She said, "We each had our own mats and little towels, and Melanie's mom is so into it, they had one of their bedrooms made into a studio. There are mirrors on one wall, which is sooo nice for checking each pose. Then, we had a neat little snack out on their deck—"

From upstairs, we heard a stream of curse words then, "Ahhh! That hurts like crazy!"

The three of us looked at each other and ran up the back stairs. Well, Mary and I ran. Gigi hadn't been cleared by her doctor to run, but she moved pretty fast for someone who was injured just a few months ago. We got to the top of the stairs to see Jamal walking up and down the hall, doing some puffy breathing. He was holding his arm, but we couldn't tell why. Mr. Shaw peeked down from the opening to the attic. "Football rears its ugly head. Dislocated his shoulder again."

Jamal grimaced. "Yeah, the glory days. Sometimes, it's the gift that keeps on giving."

I squinted at him. "Do you need to go to the emergency room?"

He blew a few deep breaths. "I'll just deal with it until I can get there so they can pop it back in."

"Ooo, ick," said Mary. "That sounds awful."

I kept my eyes on Jamal. "You want to try fixing it here first? It's sort of a yoga move."

"Really?" he said. "Just this side of voodoo, right?"

I shrugged. "Hey, it might save some time and money."

He scrunched his eyes shut, then looked at me. "All right, you're on."

I pointed to the floor. "Sit, please."

He stared at me for a second, nodded, and slid to the floor, gasping as the impact jolted his shoulder.

"Okay, pull your knees to your chest."

Jamal winced just a bit, but did what I said.

"Now, grab around your knees and point your thumbs up to the ceiling."

He took a deep breath, did it, and stared up at me.

"Okay, now lean back super slow, no jerking."

He shook his head ever so slightly, and muttered, "No jerking—what a comedian." He compressed his mouth like he was trying not to yell, and sweat beads popped out all across his forehead. Yet, as he slowly moved backwards, we could almost see the shoulder roll back into place. It wasn't exactly a pop, but pretty soon, Jamal had a big grin on his face. "Amazing. I've never done it like that before."

Gigi hugged me. "Land sakes, Emily. You might grow up to be a doctor."

"Hmm, I never thought about that idea," I said. "Actually, there's a kid on my swim team this happens to a lot if he swims too many butterfly events. A couple times when coach was busy with the divers, I watched the kid fix himself. I thought it was worth a shot."

Jamal slowly got to his feet. "I'll remember that, for sure. Been dealing with this for years. I enjoyed football, but sometimes . . ."

Mr. Shaw cleared his throat from over our heads. "Okay, we've got to get on the road pretty soon. You feel up to finishing, fella?"

Gigi said, "We'll get out of your way, gentlemen."

"Thank you, Miss Emily," said Jamal. "Sorry to interrupt your supper, ladies."

He knelt down in front of the big toolbox, massaging his shoulder. It looked as if he was waiting for us to go. That or praying, so I guessed either way that was our cue to leave. What a day!

Mary nudged me all the way down the stairs. "You have to put all these Doc Debbie things in your notes."

"Notes?" I asked.

"Yeah," said Mary, "for your Summer in the Mountains thing."

I patted my pocket. "Good idea. My notebook's right here."

She nodded. "Yup, and I bet we're all in it."

"Not everyone. You I haven't decided on yet."

"Leave me out? Never," said Mary, giggling, "Come on, we have to deliver some hangtags."

"Okay, you're definitely in," I said, running for the bikes. "But should I put you in the section marked roommate or slave driver?"

Chapter 8

Mmm-Smell That?

As we stowed our bikes at Mountain Artisans, I noticed the store van parked out front. I guess I was still staring at it when I felt a nudge from Mary. "Come on, he's about to close up."

I pushed open the shop door and heard jingling, like the bells on a sleigh at Christmas. "Ooh, listen. Wind chimes, I love these things."

Mary squeezed by me, reached over a display of hand-woven baskets and tapped one of the wind chimes. "Look, this one's made out of little whisks, like I use to whip the eggs for breakfast. When we get paid, I'm getting one. I hope it's still here."

A deep voice came from the back of the store. "I can get another one especially for you, young lady. Just leave me your name."

"You have my name," said Mary, wandering around the shop. She picked up a balsam pillow, sniffed its piney aroma and smiled. "We came to see you."

"Me?" said Evan Moss, coming toward us, brushing off his sleeves. His hair was the color of a chocolate bar, flecked with gray. Dark green eyes stared out from under bushy brows. "I was unpacking new stock, so excuse my dust." Then, recognition dawning, he blushed, and laughed. "Oh, hi, girls. I was buried in boxes."

"Sorry to bust in on you at closing time," Mary replied.

"No problem," he said, perching on a stool behind the counter. "I've got a few moments for my hangtag team."

"Yes, sir," I said, reaching into my backpack. "We're almost finished, but we wanted to make sure this was what you wanted."

Mr. Moss took the tags and studied them for a moment. "They're perfect! I love the sketch of the shop and the mountain behind it. These short phrases about the crafts and how they're made—again, perfect."

"Thanks," I said, "they take awhile to do."

He nodded. "I bet. And when they're this good, I don't mind the expense. This type of thing sets my place apart, which was why I asked Gigi if she could spare you two for a few hours every week. I'll need more for new items like the wind chimes and the teaberry-scented candles."

Mary said, "That's cool. Just give us the info. The rest of these should be to you by late tomorrow."

"Terrific," said Mr. Moss. "These are so impressive I may enlarge some and display them around the shop. That way we can feature different products. Someone else might want to hire you for artwork, Mary. And, Emily, I don't do a lot of advertising. It's crazy expensive. But if you wanted to write something about the shop, our newspaper is always looking for articles. I'll give you the contact person's name."

"Hmm," I said, "I did that for our paper back home over Christmas. I got twenty-five dollars and a gift card to the movies. Local papers seem to want stuff about the human side of retail, so I could feature some artists, and I heard you do good stuff for the community."

"Oh, it's not much. I sponsor youth leagues at the rec center and buy books for library programs."

"Well, that's great," I said. No wonder this guy was so popular around here. "Um, I'll pop by for some interviews and photos. I'll call ahead of time."

"No need," said Mr. Moss, "I'm almost always here." An odd look that lasted only a few seconds came over his face. "I prefer not to be photographed, but feel free to snap away at anything else here. That's very generous of you."

I shrugged. "Our newspaper back home might run part of it. Plus, I'll get extra credit points for English class, too."

"I should check into that for Fine Arts credit," Mary said, with a nod. "Listen, we've got another stop, and then we need to get back home."

"That Baird's Den is great. I stayed there when I first came to town. Even caught a few trout." Mr. Moss grabbed some keys, stepped to the front entrance, and flipped the sign to 'Closed.' "But, unlike other businesses, innkeeping is a 24/7 deal. I worry about Gigi. I hope it's not getting to be too much for her. I've watched her struggle to recover. The land around the inn is as valuable as a gold mine. She should keep that in mind. Maybe without some of the pressure . . ."

"That's nice of you, sir," said Mary, gathering up our stuff. "But she lives for that inn."

As we rode off toward the Y, I said, "Sounds like he really cares for Gigi."

"He does," agreed Mary. "He's grateful to Gram for the idea that made the shop go 'boom.' Her thing about smells got him thinking that aromatics could make his shop special. He started stocking good-smelling stuff that reminded people of the mountains or their childhood, and business took off."

"Pretty cool, too bad Gigi's too old for him." I cut sharply into the parking lot. "Hey, Ms. Ortiz would be perfect for Mr. Moss."

Mary nodded, parked the bike, and took off her helmet. "I know, but don't mention that to Alex. He's very protective of his mama."

"Aww, that's probably normal with a guy."

We headed into the gym, and Mary giggled. "Well, I hope this doesn't throw his game off." She tipped her head toward the bleachers. Wow, Mr. Moss must have driven like a maniac to get here before we did, and his reward was to slide into the empty seat beside Mariella Ortiz.

I shook my head. "Not much to do midweek in the mountains."

"Guess we about have to go sit by them," said Mary. "Come on."

We sat a few seats down from the couple, waved to Alex in a not crazy embarrassing way, and watched two really tall kids do a jump ball to start the game. Alex received the tip and headed up the court. Apparently he was point guard, and he moved really well with the ball. He squared off to shoot, and someone from the other team hacked the fool out of him. The ref called a foul and Alex went to the line. After the first shot touched the rim, but didn't go in, I heard Mr. Moss quietly urge, "Flip that wrist." It must have helped, because the second shot swished.

I loved basketball and could shoot well standing still. Moving fast with the ball was another story, but I was a great spectator. At the half, Ms. Ortiz called to us, "Hi, girls."

"They look good," I said.

She smiled. "I think it's the shoes."

I looked at Alex and the team huddled in a corner of the gym, swigging water and listening to their coach. "Wow, those are the 'New Blues' like the Duke team has."

Mary looked puzzled. "How did a rec team afford to get shoes like those?"

Ms. Ortiz pointed to Evan Moss. "They have a generous sponsor."

Wow, this guy's legend lived up to the hype. "Very impressive, Mr. Moss."

He smiled at all three of us. "Kids around here can always use new shoes."

We chatted a bit with Mrs. Ortiz, and when the second half was about to start, she said, "You got the bears, correct?"

Mary nodded, and said, "We did, and Gram wanted you to know she has cinnamon on order."

"Oh, thank goodness. It's so nice that Evan can import it. Some goes to Gigi and some comes to me."

"Well, we actually have lots of guests streaming in," said Mary, "so Gram will probably want more bears soon."

Mr. Moss leaned our way. "Please tell Gigi if she ever has any extras, I'll buy them from her."

Ms. Ortiz laughed, and playfully shook her finger at him. "Evan Moss, you know I only make those for Baird's Den."

"I know, but maybe Gigi would consider licensing. If we sold the official Baird's Den bears exclusively in my shop, it could make the ones she gives away more valuable."

Mrs. Ortiz thought for a moment, and then said, "Well, maybe, but it's up to Gigi. Until she changes the rules, the bears are hers."

I glanced across the gym as Alex took the floor with his team. Even though they were ahead by twenty points, he didn't appear happy. He looked up our way a few times, and I realized how hard this must be for him. Your dad dying is bad enough, but watching your mom start dating again, it's got to be kind of icky. His team continued to do well though, and pretty soon Mary nudged me.

"They've got this," she said. "I think we should split."

During the next time out, Mary waved to Alex and we slipped out the door. When we got home, Gigi was asleep but had left a note. "New guests arrive tomorrow. Two actors who have guest roles in the outdoor drama, and two semiretired ladies on their annual gem-mining trip."

I mentioned that I wasn't aware there *were* gems around here.

Mary shrugged. "Depends on who you talk to, but I went with Grandpa when I was little. We found two flecks of gold. Picture tiny pieces of shredded cheese. I still have them stashed somewhere in my closet at home. Did I find gold? Yup. Was it worth anything? Maybe five bucks. It's probably more for the hunt than the riches. You can quiz these folks and find out."

"Definitely," I said, glancing at the big vase of fresh cut lavender and roses on the entry hall table. "Gol, that smells great. Wait, do you hear me? I'm geeking out over smells. But it seems like stuff smells bigger in the mountains. Is that possible?"

Mary shrugged again. "I have no idea, but even the air seems different up here. That or we've both lost our minds. Look it up, there's your article."

Okay, so there was a lot to learn about in these mountains. I yawned and fought the urge to hit "Google." Research was just a keystroke away, but for now, zzzz.

Chapter 9

One Thing after Another

The next couple of days flashed by like time travel. My little brother has two gerbils, and I honestly felt like I was on one of their wheels. We had four guests midweek, but then two or three more found us, and we never stopped, except to sleep. The actors were super nice but kept requesting stuff. Extra pillows, a safety pin for a sleep mask, lemon in hot water, a second pot of teaberry tea. Well, they wouldn't be here forever, and the sweet thing was they gave us all tickets to one of their performances, so we had an event to put on the kitchen calendar.

The gem miners were actually easier, but when they were in the house, it was nonstop talking. Ms. Midge had grandchildren about our age, so she quizzed us like crazy about fashion tips, (okay, that was Mary she asked about those), books we liked, favorite movies, and how to download facts about gems from her computer. The other one, Ms. Beverly, trailed around after Gigi "helping." She wanted to cut flowers, organize the inn's bookshelves, and yesterday asked, "Emily, do you have any silver that needs polishing?"

I wasn't sure how to answer that, so I just said, "I don't think we actually use the silver much until around Christmas." Thankfully, that seemed to satisfy her, and she and Ms. Midge were able to accept we could get along without them while they took off for the next mine on their "must see" list.

Saturday started off pretty early with the arrival of Pete ready to do his thing to the septic tank. Mary and I were in the carriage house putting air in the bike tires when we heard a vehicle coming up the drive. "Oh, please, I know Baird's Den needs every guest it can hold, but I hope this is just someone who took a wrong turn."

Mary giggled and peeked out the door. "No worries, it's the Mountain Artisan van. Maybe Mr. Moss is here to pay us."

I put the tire gauge down and said, "A, that would be awesome. B, I never asked you about the van."

"Huh?"

"The other day, when the guys left, I noticed the sign on their vehicle was crooked."

Mary shrugged. "I guess that happens when they move the signs. Since they hardly ever drive the same vehicle twice, they use magnetic ones."

I nodded. "Ah, okay. I thought maybe they had another business, and they were covering it up."

"Nope," she said, "I don't think so. Now, turn off that curiosity mode in your head, and let's go get paid."

We headed out the door, only to be met about halfway by Mr. Moss. Mary asked, "Are you looking for us?"

"Yes, I am." He held up a shopping bag. "I brought some of the new stock to inspire you for the next batch of hangtags. And to pay up. I only walked this direction to see if the smell got worse or better."

"It gets worse," I said, pointing to the Pete's Plumbing truck, currently parked out back near the septic tank cleanout opening. "Hopefully, it won't last too much longer."

"Well, I'm sorry it came to this, but it's kind of, well, pungent," Mr. Moss said. "Where's Ms. Gigi?"

Mary said, "I'm not sure, but I'll go find her." She jogged up to the house and went in the back door.

He pointed, and we walked toward the expansive yard. "How many guests do you have this week?"

I counted on my fingers, and said, "Seven."

"Plus you three, and the occasional carpenter," he said, looking kind of serious. "Ah, here's our innkeeper. So, you went with pumping the tank?"

Grandma Gigi shoved her glasses up on her head, and sighed. "Not at first. Pete tried some strong additives, but with the inspector's visit on the horizon and your urging me to not delay the inevitable. . ." She sniffed and sniffed.

"Smart move," said Mr. Moss. "Emily said you have a packed house?"

Gigi nodded. "Yes, with only one complaint. Most of them are out and about, so that's why Pete's here now. It's just hard to hide that truck with a doily. Em has been on air freshener duty inside, and Mary took the shears, cut whatever fragrant flowers she liked the smell of, and filled any empty vases. Evan, I'd say come in, but I need to go online and check on my bank balance."

"Of course, and I won't keep you. Just remember, even a place this beautiful can be draining." He pointed at her like he was scolding a child. "You're still recovering, and we don't want you to have any setbacks. Mary promised me some time ago that you would pace yourself."

"I appreciate your concern, and I'll try to obey," grumbled Gigi. "But next time you come to visit, bring a pie, not just that highly trained nose of yours."

"Well, I learned from the best!" he said, patting her arm. "Go do what you need to do; I'll see you soon. Mary and Emily, don't rush off without your checks."

~

A little later, Pete came into the office, and said, "Well, I'm finished, and I bet with the nice breeze today, by late tonight all you'll smell out there is that pretty grass. About midweek, I'll be back to test again, and then, hopefully, you won't see me again for a couple years."

Gigi exhaled a sigh of relief. It didn't last too long, however. I paused outside the office door with Mary.

"Gracious, Pete," said Gigi, waving a piece of paper. "I thought this was going to be a good morning when you said there was no need to replace the tank, just pump it out. However, your bill is a kicker."

Pete shuffled his feet. "I did the best I could for you, Ms. Gigi. But this old tank took a lot of work. First, there was that emergency after-hours call. Then we ran some pretty sophisticated tests, followed by the additives. A place this size has a big tank. And then today, with the pump-out, disposal fees and recharging the bacteria, it all comes to a hefty sum. I discounted it as much as I could."

Gigi nodded, and pulled out the inn's checkbook. "I know, and I'm sorry to react like that. It's been an expensive summer, and we're not even to the Fourth yet. Can I pay you half now, and the rest after I make another trip to the bank?"

We scooted into the kitchen and Mary started a batch of cookies, while I fixed us some sandwiches. Pretty soon, Gigi and Pete came through the kitchen. He tipped his hat to us, and Gigi shook his hand. "Sorry I yelled, Pete. You did a wonderful job, and say 'Hi' to that sweet wife."

She watched him leave, looked at both of us, and sighed. "Good idea, Mary. The smell of cookies will scoot out any stink that's still lurking around. Em, are you making PB&Js?"

"Yes, ma'am. Would you like one?"

"I would, but first I need to get something. I'll be right back."

Mary looked up from cracking eggs into a bowl. "She's an example of how to roll with the punches, yes?"

I grinned and nodded. "Yeah, for sure."

In a few moments, Gigi came back into the kitchen, standing for a moment at the counter to do some stretches. She stretched randomly throughout the day, so we were pretty much used to it. Plus, we both had to stretch for sports, so we teased her by asking what sport or event she was going out for. It had sort of become our group joke. Like yesterday during leg stretches, she blurted out "Cross Country" and just now during back stretches she grinned impishly and said, "High Dive." When she finished, she pulled two small white envelopes from a pocket of her trail vest. "Here's one for each of you. Happy first payday, Em!"

Wow, Saturdays will never be the same. I'd gotten a small check from Mr. Moss for the first batch of hangtags, and now a big one (to me) from Gigi. "Ma'am, if you need to hold our checks for a while, that would be understandable."

She put her hands on her hips, and said, "What?"

Mary nodded. "I think she means we know it's been a rough few days for you, Gram. If it would help, we don't mind waiting to get paid."

Gigi teared up. "Well, I never. You girls are the best. No way would I do that to any employee, especially y'all. Payroll is paid out of a totally different pot, so no worries about that. The big things take a little more doing, but if we keep packing guests in here, I'll make up some ground. Thank you both, and enjoy your money. You both earned it."

"Now," I said, "let me serve you two my famous peanut butter and grape jam sandwiches, cut the fancy way, because you know that's how I roll."

Mary shook her head, and said, "Just leave mine uncut—easier to eat."

I nodded. "Personally, I like mine open faced." I held out my palm to demonstrate.

"Well, I never," said Gigi, again. "That would work great for a peanut butter and banana sandwich."

Just then, the front door chimed the arrival of new guests, and our food moment was over. But, with checks in my pocket, and a week under my belt, I was feeling pretty good. Yeah, I had to go back to work for a little while, but tonight I'd decide what color case I would get. Cell phone, here I come!

Chapter 10

Lazy Days of Summer?
Not So Much

The next day, Mary did the morning coffee prep so I could go do a guest workout with the Y swim team. It was super early so some kids could attend church and other ones could get to their weekend jobs. I loved doing it, and during the timed portion it let me know I hadn't lost all my speed. I got back to the inn grateful I had time to sweep the front porch while people were still sleeping. I was almost done when Grandma Gigi snagged me. "Em, several guests requested late checkouts, so you can't get started on rooms. Mary's working on my website so she'll be in the office. I need some help gathering more teaberry. Feel like a little hike?"

I smiled one of those inner smiles, thinking hmm, I'd biked to the Y, swum, and just swept, so "hike" was not next on my dream to-do list. But she looked so excited, how could I not go? "Sure," I said, "let me change shoes. I'll meet you out back."

No flip-flops or sandals in the woods for me, thank you very much. It wasn't bad if you wore socks, but there were crawling things in these forests up here, and I wasn't sure socks could keep them from biting me. Wuss, yes, but I hate the creepy feeling of a tick crawling up my leg. After a sprint upstairs for my hiking boots, I arrived at Gigi's side. Wow, how many pounds of teaberry leaves did we need? I looked at the two straw laundry baskets she was holding, and asked, "Are we going to fill them both?"

Gigi looked sheepish. "I get a little carried away, I know. The answer is, probably not. But we'll clip some lilacs, plus the teaberry. I thought if we each had a basket, it wouldn't be too bad for either of us. I don't want to ruin you for the day."

I grinned. "I appreciate that. Um, which way?"

Gigi pointed, and off we went. "Well, Evan's guys get back tonight. We'll have six guests, which is a nice way to end the weekend."

"For sure," I said, with a nod. "Wait, they're back already?"

"Oh, they just went to Atlanta, then maybe it was Mobile, and back they come. I expect they'll have lots of stock for the shop, and hopefully, my cinnamon sticks." She nodded toward a trail I'd never been down. "Evan imports an inexpensive type of stick from Indonesia as a favor for me. I would never use it in cooking, but it works great for the bears. "

"Wow, I'm impressed."

Gigi threw her head back and laughed. "It's just good business. My materials cost per bear is way less than if I used cooking grade cinnamon. Plus, I give some sticks to Mariella in exchange for her labor in making the bears. It's sort of a trade that lets me control the fact that only I get those little guys." She stopped, and peered around the woods. "Here we are, so let's get our clippers clicking." She made her way into a stand of low shrubs, growing randomly under taller trees and other vegetation. "See those shiny, dark green leaves? That's the teaberry bush. These little flowers will turn into berries by fall."

"Does it die off in the winter?"

"No, it's green all year." She rubbed a few leaves between her thumb and forefinger, then held it to her nose and sniffed. "That's a mountain smell to me."

I did the same thing, and while it *was* nice, it also smelled like the gum my gramps chewed. "This is what goes in that old-timey gum, right?"

Gigi nodded. "Correct, and they also use its oil for candles or potpourri. The Indian tribes used to bake pies from the berries, and oldsters chew the leaves for aches and pains. We'll steep some leaves for tea. It's not for everybody, but worth a try at least once."

I nodded, and scooted down a way to start clipping branches. For a while, all you could hear was the snip of our clippers. "Oops, we have company." Several squirrels had crept close on branches over my head, where they sat chattering. "They look like they want to jump me."

A deep voice behind us said, "They're probably just scolding you for taking their food."

We both swiveled around to face the bird guy. Weren't there other woods for him to explore?

Gigi must have read my mind. "Heavens, you startled me. We won't steal much from the squirrels."

"I was teasing," he said, "Audubon humor. We can be a little dry. Actually, what you're doing is good for the plants, so they'll make more fruit for the chipmunks who eat the teaberry fruit and the deer who eat the leaves. I'm not sure what part the squirrels eat, but they'll be happier when we're all gone."

I couldn't hold it in any longer. "Um, Audubon folks deal with birds mostly, correct?"

He nodded, and said, "Yes and no. I'm sorry, I've met Ms. Baird, but my name is Jim Adams."

"Emily Sanders, Jim," said Gigi. "One of our summer helpers."

He went on. "Audubon actually conserves and restores natural ecosystems for birds, yes, but also other wildlife."

"That's why you're always in her woods?"

"Emily, hush," said Gigi.

"Well, young lady, truth be told," said Mr. Adams, checking his watch, "we sometimes work with other agencies. Any of us who are out in the field try to mitigate any problems before they get out of hand. So, we do spot checks of local forests when we can. By the way, Ms. Baird, I noticed you have a great number of hummingbirds in your garden."

Gigi nodded. "Oh, yes, they are so fun to watch. I'd like to put up some feeders, but the bees pester them too much."

He nodded. "Well, that's what I was going to mention. I was following a Pileated Woodpecker here the other day, and I went through your property. My binoculars picked up quite a few bees on your roof."

"Wow, those must be pretty strong binocs," I blurted out.

Gigi peered at me over her sunglasses. "Well, honeybees like to be warm, so on these cool mornings, that's where they head to."

"Yes, that makes sense," he agreed. "My binocs are good, but from that distance, I thought they might be bumblebees building a nest under a loose shingle."

"Oh, heavens, that's not something we'd want at all."

"Just wanted you to be aware, ma'am." He tipped his hat. "Well, I'll be out toward the falls for the next week, so I'll trust you to watch the woods." And off he strode.

Gigi watched him go, then said, "He seems nice. Weren't you a bit hard on him?"

I shrugged. "I'm sorry, he acts nice, but that's just it. He used a lot of words, but we still don't know what he does. Mr. Adams seems like more of an actor than our new guests."

Gigi shook her head. "Maybe he's just one of those awkward, shy types and he's trying to cover that up." She looked at our baskets. "I think we're good. Not everyone likes it, and the leaves don't last all that long after they're cut."

So we headed back, chatting about boys, sports, and how I would Skype Ben tonight and tell him a bedtime story. I said, "Funny, I miss what I always complain about. He talks nonstop. I told my parents that if someone ever kidnapped him, they'd bring him back without getting the ransom, because he talked them to death."

As we entered the kitchen with our haul from the woods, Gigi said, "I know how that missing thing works. My husband smoked cigars, and I wasn't fond of them. They're messy, and kind of stinky. . ." She sighed and began stripping the leaves from the teaberry branches. Then she tossed them in a kettle, filled it with water, and set it on a burner on the stove. She motioned for me to do some, and went on. "But, when Lionel died, the thing I missed most was the aroma from those cigars."

I didn't know what to say, so I gave her a quick hug, washed my hands, and sat down to strip the teaberry leaves. "Did you say about ten leaves per serving?"

"I did," said Gigi, "and we'll make enough tea for six." She glanced up. "Melanie?"

None other than Melanie Williams was wandering the halls. "Hey, Ms. Gigi. Mary's on the phone with a potential guest, so I was peeking around to check this grand ol' place out."

Gigi nodded. "Well, there's a lot to see. You know Emily?"

Melanie beamed me a smile. "Yes, ma'am, and I hear she's been workin' real hard up here."

Why wasn't she talking *to* me instead of about me? I just kept stripping the teaberry leaves, making it pretty obvious I was working!

"And Ms. Gigi," Melanie continued, "don't forget if you need any extra helpers, I'm available."

"Yes, dear," said Gigi. "I've got your number in my book. So, you've got us loaded up with the new listing brochures? Guests often dream about buying a place up here, so that was a good idea."

"Thank you, I try," said Melanie. "If you ever decided to sell, Baird's Den would be on the cover."

"Good to know," said Gigi. "I'm still thinking about your tour idea. If you'd like to put something down on paper, like a map of where you'd go, how much you would charge and other info, I'd be glad to look it over. Then we'll chat. Email it if you like, and that can save you a trip."

"Oh, it's no trouble to just pop by, so I'll be back. Okay if I leave through the back?" And, with a half pirouette on pink leather sandals, she left with a little whiff of her signature Ice Pop cologne drifting over the kitchen.

"She's different," I said.

"And," said Gigi, "apparently, she'll be back."

A bit later found me, Mary, Gigi, and Andre from the drama sipping tea on the front porch. Mary and I crooked our little fingers and pretended to be fancy society ladies, which was a stretch with us sitting there in jean shorts. I have to say, teaberry tea smelled way better than it tasted, but Mary vowed it got better every time she had it. We clinked cups together about the time the Mountain Artisan guys pulled up the driveway in a silver minivan.

As they came up the steps, Gigi held up the teapot. "You two are just in time."

Jamal shivered and said, "Thank you ma'am, but teaberry is an acquired taste that I personally don't know if I'll ever acquire!"

Mr. Shaw grinned. "I'll have some, ma'am. But first, I'm hunting for a couple tools I might have left here. May I check the area we were working in the other night?"

Gigi nodded. "Of course. You know the way. Are you two headed toward the shop?"

Jamal nodded. "We are, and we have a ton of stuff to unload. Your spice order is somewhere in the pile."

"It'll be worth the wait. Mary, can you get them a key so if they pull a late-nighter, they can still get in here after hours?"

Mary said, "I'll have it when you come back down."

And I said, "Hey, we'll even save you some tea to have with your bedtime cookie snack."

"You're too kind, Ms. Emily," said Jamal, nodding to Andre. "Enjoy your evening, folks."

Andre finished the last of his tea and said, "That's my cue to get my partner up from her nap and get us headed to work too. Curtain goes up promptly at 8:00 whether we're in place or not."

I smiled one of those mostly inner smiles. Interesting summer; I keep getting more stuff to write about, like a strange tea you make with leaves from a forest, and behind the scenes interaction with real working actors. Oh, yeah, and septic tanks. Maybe not headline worthy, but definitely interesting!

Chapter 11

Bee Gone!

By Tuesday, the smell in the yard was gone, and when Pete tested the tank, everything was perfect. He and Gigi actually slapped hands when he came inside to give her the news.

After witnessing that, Mary nudged me and said, "Okay, Gram. We're gonna get on with changing sheets." We headed upstairs.

Gigi was all about efficiency, so she told me from day one that changing sheets would go faster if we tag-teamed them. It was fun, and we had it down to just a few minutes per bed.

Mary peeked out the upstairs hall window. "Alex is out there trimming, so expect him to swipe some cookies when he's done mowing."

I nodded. "He's funny, just slides in the back door, washes his hands, and the only thing else you hear is the glass lid of the cookie jar clinking."

Mary smiled. "Yeah, he's easy to have around. Not like some guys who always want to show off or act stupid."

We attacked twin beds in the first room. "I'm surprised he doesn't show off more. I think he likes you."

"Really?" Mary said, blushing slightly. "I hadn't noticed."

"Then, you're blind, missy." I scooped up the dirty sheets and tossed them in a pile outside the next room.

We finished all the beds, and Mary headed downstairs, saying she needed to start a new batch of cookies. Hm, I thought; she hadn't noticed anything, huh? I had grabbed cleaning stuff and fresh towels from the supply closet when I heard a yell. I peeked out a window toward the backside of the inn. From there, I could see Alex holding his neck and pointing to the top of Baird's Den. I ran down the stairs and outside. "What happened?"

Mary was standing next to Alex, wringing out a wet dishtowel she must have grabbed from the kitchen. She handed it to him and said, "He got stung by a bee."

"Aw, shoot." I looked where he had pointed, and saw a bunch of bees actually flying into the wooden cupola on the roof. "Wow, think they're from the garden?"

"I guess," said Mary. "Where else would they be from?"

Just then, Gigi appeared. "I was on the phone with the bank. I heard someone yell. Alex, what's wrong with your neck?"

He removed the cloth to show her an impressive red welt, and tipped his head toward the top of the inn. "See up there? New visitors, ma'am."

Gigi peered up and gasped. "Oh, my goodness. A swarm of bees! Jim Adams mentioned some were around the roof, but I thought they were just getting warm on a cool morning. Alex, are you allergic? Do we need to get you to the hospital?"

He shook his head. "Naw, I'm not allergic, just mad. I was trying to slip in and swipe some cookies. When it stung me, I yelled, so it was like the dumb bee ratted me out."

"Well, I'm calling the exterminator," grumbled Gigi. "I hate hurting the bees, but I can't have guests and my dear employees in danger."

Just then, Clayton Shaw popped his head around the corner of the inn. "Ma'am, sorry to bother you."

Gigi smiled. "No bother, Clayton. It's just one of those mornings when you wonder why you ever wanted to be a business owner. What can I help you with?"

"I'm just letting you know we're heading to DC tonight, and we'll be back by the first of the week."

"Goodness, y'all are busy. We'll be looking for you," Gigi said, with a wave. "Gotta get a call into the exterminator."

"Mice?"

"Bees."

Mr. Shaw grimaced. "Honey bees?"

Gigi nodded. "Yes." She pointed toward the roof.

"That's a shame. But, killing 'em might be the right way to go with the danger of anaphylactic shock and all. Bee stings can be deadly."

"Well," said Gigi, "yes. I really have the safety of my guests to consider, and if that inspector gets wind of this, he could shut us down. I don't see that I have much choice."

"Really?" asked Alex. "I thought you liked having bees around, for the garden and all."

"I do," replied Gigi, "but I don't want them in the attic."

Mary looked at me and whispered, "Any ideas?"

I snapped my head around and said, "Actually, yes. Before you call an exterminator, are there any beekeepers around? Maybe they can just move the hive."

"How do they do that?" asked Mary.

"Remember that kid in my science class? He showed us this smoker thingy, and did a PowerPoint on how they do it."

Mr. Shaw nodded. "Well, it's going to cost you either way. Good luck."

"Bye, Clayton," Gigi sighed, and turned toward the inn. "Let me see if I can find one of those bee folks, and if they take credit cards. My cash flow has slowed to a trickle with all these unforeseen expenses. Kids, wrangle some guests if you see any."

~

Wrangle? Mary and I weren't really sure what that meant, but we decided to go to town and talk up the inn. We printed some new brochures, wore our Baird's Den T-shirts, and hoped our marketing blitz would pay off. We left brochures all around town, ending our tour with some for Mountain Artisans. Plus, we had to turn in our latest hangtags, and I needed to schedule a time with Mr. Moss to start my interview. But the only person in the shop was Ms. Ortiz, and guess who she was talking to? The bird guy! We looked around for a few minutes, until, tipping his hat like always, he smiled at Alex's mom and walked out the door.

Ms. Ortiz fluffed her hair and grinned at us. "Well, I think I just made a sale!"

"Of what?" asked Mary.

"If I can come up with a bird design, the Audubon Society might want some balsam pillows. And maybe bird or animal-motif dishtowels, for the baking kits."

"Which, by the way, are super cute," I said, unpacking the sample ones from my backpack. "After I get my phone money saved up, I'm buying the muffin kit for my mom."

Ms. Ortiz nodded. "It's cute, but I'm partial to the other one. It has the best flour around for making pie crusts."

I nodded, pretending to understand that one brand of flour could be better than another. "Um, is Mr. Moss in the back?"

"Nope, he's over at the Tennessee store."

"He's got two stores?" I asked. "Wow."

"I know," she sighed, "business is booming. I'm exhausted, but it's a good feeling."

"Will he be around on Friday?"

Ms. Ortiz checked the calendar, and nodded. "I'm working at home Friday, so he'll be here in the shop for sure."

"Could you let him know I'll be by to start my interview?"

"Will do, and Mary, thanks for the brochures. Remember, Christmas in July isn't far off. I'm already making ornaments for the tree. Cinnamon stick bundles, balsam trees, and cute little baskets filled with holly, so come back soon."

We got back to the inn to find that the inspector had showed up, apparently making a surprise visit. He clomped all through the house, picking away at the tiniest things, but it was obvious Grandma Gigi had done everything he'd requested. He'd almost finished, when the Blackstone Beekeepers vehicle pulled up. Uh-oh, I thought.

A petite lady dressed in a khaki shirt, jeans, and hiking shoes hopped out of the driver's seat and strode up the front steps. Mary and I put the bikes away and all but ran around to the front porch. This ought to be interesting.

Inspector Milton had come through the house from the kitchen, tapping the clipboard and pointing at Gigi, when he saw the newest arrival at the door.

"Hi," said the lady, "I'm Barb Blackstone, and I think I'm here to wrangle some bees."

Aha, I thought. Apparently wrangling was a very popular activity around here.

"Bees?" asked the inspector.

Gigi sighed. "Yes, Silas. I think we've got an active hive somewhere on the third floor, which is basically the attic."

"Maybe so, but that still puts any of your guests who are allergic to bees potentially in harm's way. This is not a positive mark for you, Ms. Baird."

"Well," said Ms. Blackstone, "she's taking action to shed this structure of bees in a very environmentally friendly way, and I'm one of the best beekeepers in the mountains."

"That may be true, but I may need to check with my superiors about closing the inn until it's safe for guests."

Gigi gasped. "Oh, no, this is my livelihood. These bees are nowhere near any guest rooms."

Ms. Blackstone asked, "How many guests are here tonight?"

A surprised look came over Gigi's face. "Actually, the last two just checked out. I haven't any reservations until Friday night."

"Perfect! Sir, I may have all these bees out of here by tomorrow. So, how about we exchange business cards, and I'll keep you apprised of my work here." She was a really cute blonde lady, fortyish, with a very winning smile.

The inspector tried to stay grumpy, but he finally shrugged and said, "I'll be waiting to hear from you, Ms. Blackstone. Good day, all."

Gigi nodded at the inspector and swung the door wide open for the beekeeper. "Right this way, Ms. Blackstone."

"Oh, it's Barb, and just point me to where you think the bees are. I'll be back and forth getting a few pieces of equipment, but once I know something I'll come get you. First, though, let me check outside so I can get a bead on where they might be entering. Can one of you young ladies guide me?"

I nodded and said, "Sure, come on. My name's Emily."

Mary said, "Cool, and I'll help Gram get dinner on the table. I'm starved."

Ms. Blackstone pulled out a tripod and a camera with a telephoto lens on it. I pointed out where we'd seen bees, and she started snapping photos. "Emily, if you would show me the approximate spot where this is on the inside, you can go have dinner."

We found the area, and I left her working. She was strong, hauling ladders and bags of equipment up two flights of stairs. Finally she finished and came to find Gigi with us in the kitchen. I slurped the last of my second bowl of gazpacho and nibbled on a roll.

Ms. Blackstone said, "Well, it's an active hive of honeybees, and if you didn't have that inspector breathing down your neck, I'd tell you to leave them in place. They're fun to watch, and you could get some honey for the inn. But I know you don't want to take any chances, so I can mix a little concoction to catch the swarm. It might take two tries to get every one, but then you should be okay. The thing is, if you don't want your garden bees to do this again, you'll need to have a carpenter block off the area I'm taking the swarm from."

"So," said Gigi, "you think this group came from their friends in my garden?"

Ms. Blackstone nodded. "Most likely, but I'll know more after my capture is complete. So, am I free to corral these bees?"

Gigi nodded, and said, "Bee my guest! Get it, girls?"

Mary hugged Gigi, and said, "Cute, Gram, but you'd best give up your dream of stand-up comedy, and stick to innkeeping!"

Hours later, the beekeeper lady took a large white bucket with a lid on it to her truck. She explained, "I enticed them with sugar water, and then every little while knocked the wall to get their attention. Then, slowly almost all of them let loose and dropped into the bucket. I'll take this bunch away, make sure I got the queen, install them in a proper hive, and label it Baird's Den. Perhaps you can visit it and we'll share some honey."

"Oh, that would be wonderful," said Gigi. "What do I owe you?"

"Nothing tonight," said Ms. Blackstone. "I need to do a clean sweep tomorrow in the daylight to confirm they all left with me. You can call your carpenter in, and then I'll give you my bill."

She held up her hand. "And, because you catch more flies with honey"—her bright blue eyes twinkled at all three of us—"I'll copy Mr. Inspector on my report to you. It will commend you for your contribution to the environment by saving an active bee hive and how by doing so, you harmed no guests and saved a bunch of bees."

"Bless your heart, Barb," said Gigi. "I'll still have two strikes against me as far as the inspector is concerned."

"Yes, but Ms. Gigi," I said, "with this 'do-gooder' stuff, I bet all you get is a warning and a thank you. Hey, we might even be able to get a mention in the paper."

"There you go," said Ms. Blackstone. "That's the reason people should always have kids around—they originated the positive spin."

Chapter 12

Hook, Line, and No Worms Needed

On Thursday morning Gigi headed for her last physical therapy appointment, and Mary went with her. The therapist planned to cover more advanced stretching techniques, and Mary thought she could use some of them for gymnastics.

As they left, Gigi said, "The bee lady gave us the green light, so Lyle's back today to board up the place in the attic where the bees were. We should be back by the time he finishes. Have fun in the pantries!"

I glanced up at all the shelves before me. Gigi had asked if I would re-arrange the cans by expiration date and sizes. Besides that, there were supplies of different sized storage bags, candles, paper towels, paper plates, napkins, and seasonal decorations. She'd said this was an ongoing project, and with pantries this massive, I could see why. The thing was,

I loved rearranging stuff. I didn't go loco alphabetizing cans by their product or anything, but I did like stuff to line up and make sense. My mom would say my room was almost always filthy (like little puffs of dust bunnies around), but at least it was tidy and organized. So, since it was also raining, this wasn't a horrible way to spend the rest of the morning.

I'd been at it a couple hours when Mr. Holton came downstairs carrying a ladder and his toolbox. He set that stuff in the hallway, went back upstairs, and came right back down carrying something else. I was thinking about where to put the candle supply, as there must have been fifty or sixty of them, maybe for during a power outage? Anyway, I finally realized Mr. Holton was standing in the doorway, "waiting nicely" as my mom always asks Ben to do.

"Yes, sir?"

"Any idea how much longer Ms. Gigi will be?" he asked.

I looked at him and smiled. "It should be any minute. They're too nice to say anything, but I think they get nervous if the newbie's in charge for very long."

He chuckled, and said, "Well, you look like you have things under control."

"I really can't get in too much trouble in a pantry. Oops, there they are."

Gigi and Mary came into the kitchen carrying a couple bags, and unloaded fresh strawberries, broccoli, and tomatoes from the farmers' market. "Oh, good, Lyle, you're all finished? If you have a bill for me, I'll get you a check as soon as I can."

Mr. Holton nodded. "I left it for you on the office counter, and there's no hurry with paying. I've finished closing up the area where the bees were, and your beekeeper did a nice job up there, so I was surprised to see this." He held up a plastic milk jug with the top cut out and a couple nails dangling from it. "That keeper was very thorough, and I just thought it was odd she didn't throw this out. It's sticky and probably had something to do with moving the hive."

I nodded. "Right. They use sugar water to calm the bees down. I saw a container when she was bringing everything up from her work van, but hers was a glass jar, like the ones my grandma uses for canning vegetables. With the metal top that screws on?"

Mr. Holton nodded. "A Mason jar. Well, that would be what I'd expect. But, this thing was nailed between the studs of the side wall where the hive was."

Gigi sighed and wrote something on a piece of paper. "I don't know why it was there, and honestly, there's just too much to think about lately. Here's her number. I'm sure she can tell you what this was for, or even if it was hers."

Mr. Holton shrugged, and we all stood there kind of awkwardly.

I finally said, "Ms. Gigi, I bet Mr. Holton is super busy with work for all the summer folks. Since I helped the bee woman, want me to call her?"

Gigi said, "Well, sure. That would be great. Thanks for everything, Lyle."

Mary seemed to want to speak with Mr. Holton, and I had a bag of trash for the dumpster, so we walked him out. She said, "I'm sorry, I just think this all is stressing Gram out, and she doesn't want us to know it."

"I think you're right," he said. "Keep an eye on her, and let me know what you find out."

~

The next day Gigi seemed in much better spirits, as she had decreed it was Fly-Fishing Friday. As soon as our morning inn stuff was done, Mary and I took off to meet Alex at the stream. Thanks to Gigi's bribe of a container of cookies, he'd agreed to teach us how to fly-fish. Honestly, I thought from the way he acted when Mary was around, he'd have done it for free.

Mary obviously had some idea what fly-fishing entailed, since she wore a khaki shirt, dark green shorts, a camo scarf, and a big bucket hat. Me? About the only thing I wore that was appropriate was my dark wash cut-off shorts and hiking boots. My white baseball hat and bright blue shirt were apparently no-nos in fly-fishing as you wanted to blend in with the woods. That was another issue for me. I'd wade-fished a lot at the coast, and from boats on the lake. However, I'd never tried to fling a line standing on the bank of a stream in a forest. Tree branches and rocks were everywhere!

Alex gave us each a rod and me two flies. Mary already had some of Grandpa Baird's hooked onto the pocket of her shirt. I copied that with one of my flies, and attached the other one to the leader thingy.

Alex then showed us how to pull some line out and sweep the rod toward the water. We tried flicking our wrists, but we couldn't get a clear space to stand side by side and not wham into each other or get snagged on a low hanging branch. "Em, why don't you move up nearer to the log bridge, and Mary can stay here. It's good you both have sunglasses on, but unless they're polarized, I don't know if you'll be able to see the fish very well."

"What are we fishing for?" I asked.

"Trout—rainbow if we're lucky, or maybe some brookies."

"Do we need a license?" asked Mary.

"Nope, not until we're sixteen," said Alex, pointing at Mary's wrist. "Pull it back over your head, then bring it forward fast, and aim it out like to ten o'clock. The line and the fly should kind of be in a straight line right out in front. Tug and pull a few times. Em, can you do that from up there?"

I pouted, and said, "Not when I keep snagging a rock or a rhododendron bush. Can I get in the water?"

"Sure," Alex said, "but before you do that, do a roll. That's like a 'half-cast.' Don't let the rod go behind your head, just stop when it's straight up, then flick it forward. You shouldn't get tangled in the branches that way. You can wade, but ¡Aguas! Be careful, keep your weight balanced between your feet, and don't go out too far. The good thing is this stream is so clear, you can see any deep holes before you step in them."

Mary looked over at me and said, "Watch out for algae or moss on the rocks. It makes them so slippery."

I tried to cast again. "Aha! Look, it went in the water way out in front of me."

Alex moved down the way, flicking and flinging his little green fly so fast I couldn't see it. He got a couple bites, but no fish. Mary changed her fly to a different color, which matched her outfit. She declared the new fly would catch "the big one" and eventually, it did—a brookie all of seven inches long. We took her picture with him, and then she released him into the stream. An hour for one fish might seem like a big waste of time, but it actually was fun, in a frustrating, learning kind of way. I loved watching Alex flick the rod like a ringmaster.

"You two like it?" asked Alex. "It's kind of a challenge. These fish are pretty smart."

"Yeah," muttered Mary. "I'll practice this in the yard, and come back for the big one."

"That's actually a great idea," nodded Alex. "How much time do we have?"

Mary clomped up the bank, leaned the rod against a tree, and checked her phone. "Gram texted me a little while ago and needs me to come back soon and watch the office. She's got to pick up a prescription. Why did you ask?"

Alex held up a bucket and shook it, making whatever was in there clunk around.

"You brought marbles to the woods?" I asked.

"Nope," he said, prying off the lid. "Rocks. Smooth, perfect flat river rocks."

"Hah," I said, "I will win this battle, kiddos."

Mary looked puzzled, then grinned. "Oh, no way. I won the regional Girl Scout rock-skipping badge four times in a row."

"There's no badge for that," Alex said, handing us each a paper cup of stones. "Is there?"

Mary flung her first one, which went almost all the way across the river. "Nope, but there should be."

I followed, and only made six skips. Alex took his turn. We heard a single sploosh, and knew he'd thrown a dud. We laughed so hard Mary nearly fell backwards into the stream. Neither of us ever skipped our stones as far as she did, so she ended up staff rock-skipping champ for the day. We said she had an advantage since she was closer to the ground. She was about to zing some height jokes of her own when her phone chirped.

It was Gigi, so Mary took off while Alex and I gathered the stuff up. I was taking a swig of water when out of the corner of my eye I saw Mr.

Adams stride by. I poked Alex with one of the fishing rods and pointed. "Let's see where he's headed." I grabbed the rods, while Alex carried the bucket and empty fishing creel. We didn't get too far before we spotted Adams coming right at us on the trail.

"Hello, kids! Didn't mean to ignore you, but I'm tracking a piping plover."

"Here in Gigi's woods?" I asked.

"Well, not exactly," he said. "I'm just using the Baird's Den trails to get through to the land trust tract. Sort of just cutting through."

Alex said, "Don't you need a special permit to enter the land trust property?"

Mr. Adams looked off into the woods and fiddled with the strap on his camera, which had the biggest telephoto lens I'd ever seen. "Hmm? Oh, I have the permit."

All I could think of was, then why didn't you enter through the front of their land? I wasn't sure if Alex knew this, but a plover is a shore bird. Why the heck was Adams tracking a bird that belonged on the Outer Banks of North Carolina? "Well, we've got to get back to work, sir. Good luck with finding the bird."

"What?" he asked, still peering into the woods. "Oh, yes. Thanks."

We took off toward the inn, and when we got a ways down the trail, I said, "Was that strange?"

"I guess." Alex shrugged. "Apparently, I have to stay neutral on all things Adams. He asked my mom out on a date."

"Oh, wow. That's got to be weird."

"Yeah, I guess. She seemed excited about it, so I'll let you know how things shake out."

We walked a ways in silence, and then he said, "Does Mary like movies?"

I tapped him on the head with the tip of one of the fishing rods. "Why? Did you want to double-date?" I ducked as Alex pretended to punch me, and thought, guys are as confused about the whole dating thing as we are. "Seriously? She's a movie fiend!"

When Alex and I got back to the inn, Mary reminded me I was supposed to do the Moss interview today. I washed up, changed shoes, threw on a dressier shirt, and took off for town. I pedaled along, wondering if real journalists ever rode their bikes to interviews.

As I got to the shop, I also wondered if real journalists did interviews in shorts and sneakers. Hopefully, that was a yes, so I pushed open the door and I caught a whiff of pie—lemon meringue. Aw, my mom makes the best one ever, and for an instant I was back in our Virginia kitchen. Instead, I all but stumbled into Melanie Williams, who was wrapping a pie and one of Ms. Smith's pretty floral arrangements for a customer. Wow, I hadn't been here in a few days, and look who happened!

"I'll be right with you," Melanie sang out. She finished with the lady and beamed her smile at me. "How'd I do? It's my second day!"

I shrugged. "Good, from what I saw. So are you working here?"

Melanie shook her head. "Nope, just volunteering. He hired somebody for part-time, but they can't start until next week. Mr. Moss said if I'd help him out a few hours this week, he'd make a donation to my cheer squad."

"Seems like a win-win to me," I said, nodding. "Um, is he in the back? I'm supposed to interview him for a newspaper article. Okay if I just head that way?"

"No one is allowed back there, not even me," Melanie said, sort of puffing up. "Aren't you kind of young to write for a newspaper?"

Grr, Mary might like her, but this chick was annoying. "The editor of your local paper doesn't seem to think so."

"Well, *now* I get it. I'll tap on the door and let him know you're here."

I started checking out the newest soaps, potpourris and lotions. I had to admit, even though this stuff was expensive, the smells were amazing.

I was so lost in whiffs of lavender and bubble gum that I didn't notice Mr. Moss until he was surprisingly close to me. "What's your favorite, Emily?"

I jumped "Wow, I didn't hear you coming. Quiet shoes."

He nodded. "So you like this new line?"

"Yes," I said, nodding and holding up my notebook. "First, where do you find all this stuff? Some of it seems pretty unique."

He pointed to the bench out front, and we headed that way. "You know I started with local crafts, and thanks to Ms. Gigi, added the scents. By the way, how is she? I'm so glad she got you kids to help out this summer, but that inn is so much for her to handle."

I shrugged, not really knowing what to say. "Well, she seems to be doing okay. I'll tell her you asked about her."

"Please do. Now, where was I? Oh, yes. Then, I was approached about international products. I brought some in, but for some reason, by the time they arrived they smelled funny. Mariella suggested displaying the foreign things with some of the aroma-based products. Now I store, display, and package that way, and the makers of products like that bubble gum smelling soap find *me*."

"Awesome," I said, sitting on the bench and peeking at my question list. "Where are you from?"

"Well, I grew up in New Jersey, but I've lived all over. Miami, Houston, Baltimore."

"How did you end up in Winton?"

"Real estate. I'd sold property in Florida, and needed to invest the money. The mid-Atlantic area seemed ripe for business, and I'd vacationed nearby. There were some condo bargains here, so I'm living in one and might renovate another."

"Are your guys helping with that project?"

"My guys?" said Mr. Moss, with an odd tone in his voice. "What do you mean?"

"Well, they carry tools with them."

"They do, don't they?" he blurted out, and then quickly sort of covered that question. "Sure, when I stop running them ragged, that's exactly what they'll be doing. Odd you noticed tools."

I shrugged. "Not really. I'm kind of geeky observant. My mom calls it being nosy, but my English teacher said it was a good trait for a writer." I held up my notebook. "Speaking of that, you're offering pies now?"

He grinned. "Surprised you, huh? Becca Bakes is supplying the shop with pies, the smell of which is irresistible to shoppers. And having them promotes the baking kits."

"Okay, I get the pies, but muffin pans and flour don't have that smell factor."

Mr. Moss said, "Well, thanks to Mariella again. Her dishtowels are extraordinary partly because they're made from antique linens, but that made them pricey. When I found the spatterware items, she suggested a baking bundle, a pan, a towel, and ingredients like a mix or flour.

Quality flour has a nice aroma. And just *seeing* baking ingredients can make people feel like they've just had a whiff of Grandma's homemade bread or muffins. Smells can stick with humans over fifty years."

"Awesome info." I made some notes. "Um, do you have any hobbies?"

"Oh, I rarely get away from the shops. But I enjoy golf, reading mysteries, and volunteering. Mountain Artisans sponsors several youth sports teams, so I catch some of those games when I can."

"Do you have any pets?"

"No, but I'm considering a cat for the shop. The muffin mixes seem to attract mice. When we have the cedar trees, we're okay because they hate cedar. Mice don't like cinnamon either, so I've tied bundles of the sticks together and hung them around the shop. But I don't want to have too much of one particular aroma. So, I'm also looking at a line of essential oils like peppermint or lemongrass."

"Also cool. Um, I might have more questions, but right now that's it. Oops, other than Tennessee, do you have more shops?"

"No, just these two. But I sell our crafts and products to lots of other stores. We have things in ten different states."

"Wow, that explains why your guys stay on the road a lot."

He tipped his head to a passerby, then spoke. "Well, they're an important part of my distribution structure. They service my current accounts, and show potential new customers the quality of our products."

"Sounds like a good idea," I scooped up my stuff, and stuck out my hand. "Thank you so much for your time."

"You're welcome," said Mr. Moss, peering over the top of his sunglasses. "Of course, you will let me see the piece before you submit it?"

"Sure, sir," I agreed, "no problem. I'll be back anyway to take some photos of the crafts. See you soon."

I waved to Melanie and headed toward the inn. My best friend from home, Leanne, had emailed me the other day, told me what she'd been doing, and asked if I'd had any adventures yet. Hmm, instead of going to summer school, I'd goofed around in a trout stream today. Also, I didn't have to babysit like her, and got to interview a prominent businessman. Adventures? Maybe not to some kids, but to me Fly-Fishing Friday was a huge thumbs-up.

Chapter 13

Looking from a Different Angle

Saturday, I was on duty in the office when the phone rang. It was Alex, and I said, "Aw, Mary's not here. She's at the Y."

He said, "I know, and she's part of the reason I can't practice free throws."

I nodded. "Oh, right, she's helping at the gymnastics camp. So, they're using the whole gym?"

"Yup, they are, so I was wondering if I could come by a little later and use the rim on the back of the carriage house for a while."

"Well, sure," I said, "I didn't even know one was back there."

"Been there forever," he said. "Do I need bug spray?"

"Nah, the bee lady did her magic. Hey, could we take a look at the nails you found? You know I saved them."

"Sure, but I don't think they'll look any different, unless they've started rusting."

"I know, but I'd appreciate it. So come on." As we hung up I shrugged, thinking no, the nails won't look any different, but Mary won't be here fussing about how crazy I am.

The bell on the front door jingled, so I hopped up only to hear, "It's just me!"

I plastered on my "public smile" and waved from the office. "Hi, Mel."

She peeked over the little counter and said, "Is Ms. Gigi around?"

"Not right now," I replied.

"Oh, rats," said Melanie, holding up a manila envelope. "I put all my ideas for the walking tour on paper and wanted to run it past her."

I nodded. "Well, that won't work today, but why not leave it so she can check it out? Then she'll call you with any questions."

Somehow, I knew that wouldn't be adequate, and sure enough, Melanie opened the envelope and yanked out some of the plans. "How about I show you what I had in mind and you can fill her in?"

"Mel, I'll give it a quick peek, but I'm all by myself here right now..."

She giggled. "No problemo, I'll be super quick!" And, with a grand gesture, she spread everything out. There was a little guide to the stops on the tour, a map, quirky facts about Winton, and suggested pricing. It was impressive. Apparently there was a brain hiding under that hair.

"How often would you do this?"

She made a face. "That's the one thing I don't really have an answer for. What do you think?"

"Off the top of my head, maybe start small and see how it goes. Like try once during the week and once on the weekend?"

She grabbed a pen from the counter, and carefully printed "Suggested Tour Times" on the back of one of the pages. "Do you have a sticky?"

I produced a purple one and she smiled in thanks, pressing it on the page. She bit her lip. "So, you think it sounds okay?"

It pained me to say this, but I had to be honest. I nodded. "Actually, it's way better than okay. I'm surprised there's nothing like this already here."

She giggled again, then jumped up and down a little. "Me too. Thanks, Emily. So, you'll be sure and show this to Ms. Gigi?"

I gave her a look and a thumbs-up.

"Okay, sorry—I get carried away." She waved like she was in a parade, then blessedly took off.

I packed her packet back together and grabbed the phone. Ten minutes later, I finished a reservation and looked up.

Gigi peeked in the office doorway. "I had the most wonderful walk, and my back feels the best it has in weeks. There must be something to that stretching stuff. Everything quiet here?"

I nodded. "Yes, and no. Melanie was here with all her tour info for you."

"Well, I've got to say, she's persistent."

"Yeah, that's for sure," I agreed. "And, for some reason, she drives me crazy." I grabbed the tour packet. "But, Gigi, this is really cool. She knocked it out of the park."

"Wow," said Gigi, "high praise. I'll give it a look this afternoon."

"Great," I said. "And Alex called and wanted to use the basketball rim behind the carriage house."

"Yikes," said Gigi, "it's been forever since anyone used that thing. I'd forgotten it was there. He might want someone to guard him, so I'll take a quick shower and come relieve you for awhile."

"Fantastic," I said, walking upstairs with her. "I need to grab something from our room, but I'll scoot right back."

After I returned to the office, the phone continued to stay quiet, but one couple stopped by to drop off their luggage before they picked up their friends for golf. I chatted them up, gave them a little bag of cookies and said we looked forward to seeing them later. By the time Alex pedaled up the driveway, Gigi had come to relieve me. I handed her Mel's packet and went outside.

Alex leaned his bike against a tree and undid a mesh bag from his handlebars. Fishing out a basketball, he held it up and said, "It's okay with her, yes?"

I nodded. "Of course, and I've got the nails."

"Why'd you want me to see them?"

"I can't shake loose of them."

"Okay, but not right yet," he said, pointing to the path that looped around the carriage house. "How's Gigi feeling?"

"She's doing great. Just taking her meds now and then, and started stretches in her rehab. Plus, she just got back from a walk. Why?"

"When she first got hurt, she seemed so spaced out sometimes, I'd check on her whenever I came over to work in the yard."

"She fell down the basement stairs, right?" I asked.

"Not the whole way down," he said, clanging his next shot off the rim. "The way she told it to me, the light on the stairs kept flickering and she said it was just annoying, and she's short, so couldn't reach the bulb. Finally, one night it was burned out and she said that made her so happy, because at least it wasn't flickering. She was holding a flashlight and the laundry basket, and got off balance. I think she skidded down the last five or six steps."

I shuddered. "I guess that was after her team left?"

"Yeah," he nodded, "right after. What a gig for the Becks—teaching summer school in China. Good for me too, because that's how I got the lawn account here. Anyway, at first Ms. Gigi had a nurse here for a few weeks, and then Mary came. When the nurse started staying here at night, she and Ms. Gigi asked me to change the bulb over the steps. I did, but there was nothing wrong with it."

"Really?" I said. "What was it?"

He shrugged. "I don't know, but it just took twisting the bulb in tight, and it blazed right on." He eyed the rim. "Okay, I got to get rollin' here. Coach wants us to shoot one hundred free throws each day. It goes way faster if someone rebounds for me. You available?"

I nodded, thinking the faster this went, the sooner he'd help me. We sort of got in a rhythm. Most of his shots went in, so I caught the ball under the hoop and passed it back to him. When he missed, I ran down the rebound. It wasn't long, and he'd made his daily total.

"Nails?" Alex asked.

I patted my pocket.

"Come on."

I followed him inside the carriage house to the late Mr. Baird's table. I wasn't sure when Gigi's husband died, but things looked like he'd just stepped out for a moment. Eyeglasses leaned against the microscope on the table, and several different sized magnifiers stuck out of the pencil cup beside it. I got some paper from a tray and grabbed a pencil. "Questions: 1) Are these nails from the board that hit Mr. Blanton? 2) How did they come out of the board? 3) Why would someone do that? You use the microscope and I'll use the magnifying glass."

Alex pulled a tissue from his pocket and reached to clear the dust off the microscope.

"Stop," I warned. "No tissues."

"Why? Always need 'em for my stupid allergies."

"Okay, sorry," I said, feeling bad for anyone who has to blow their nose a lot. "No good on a lens. We need cloth."

He grabbed the bottom of his T-shirt, grinned, and wiped off the glass.

I spread the nails out on the table. I blew specks of dust off the largest magnifying glass, and used it to inspect the nails. They both were curved a little and not very rusted. The edges of each head were slightly curled up like a little cup. I waited quietly for Alex to finish with his two nails.

He looked at me. "I'm guessing these were helped out of the board with a hammer. May I see yours?"

I handed mine over and waited. "It's the same cupping on the tops, right?"

He nodded and held up a piece of paper like it was a board. With his other hand, he pretended to tap underneath the board with a hammer. "All four of the tips are slightly blunted, like someone knocked them up and out."

I grinned. "Ah, I missed that, but I see it now. So, that's the answer for Question Two. What about Questions One and Three?"

Alex shook his head. "We're pretty certain the nails came from the step that hit Mr. Blanton but can't be absolutely sure, so that's Question One, but why? That's a puzzle. It sure as heck wasn't a good prank because someone got seriously hurt."

I nodded. "Agreed, but just think about the past couple weeks. And forget what Mary says because this is not my imagination running wild. We've had the step, the bees, and the septic tank. Maybe it's just a huge run of bad luck, but what if it isn't?"

Alex bounced the basketball and looked kind of bored. "Em, the bees found their way in from the garden, and the septic tank's gotten a lot of use lately."

"Mr. Holton found a plastic container of sugar mixture nailed into the rafters. The bee lady used glass jars, and took everything with her. This was kind of hidden where she didn't see it. And I smelled chlorine upstairs at the inn not long before the septic tank tanked. Counting these nails, that's three strange things right here under our noses."

Alex spun the basketball around and around on one of his fingertips, then passed me the ball. "Maybe it's four."

I wanted to try that spinning thing, but instead said, "Four?"

"It's possible the bulb in the basement I messed with for Ms. Gigi could have worked its own way loose."

"Huh?" I asked. "What do you mean?"

"Okay, you know the light bulbs in the basement are the old-school kind with the filament inside. They get hot and the base expands, then they cool off and it contracts. So, the bulb could potentially loosen itself a little bit, and eventually it could be enough to cause it to flicker. On the other hand, maybe someone loosened the bulb so the stairs would be dark."

"Eew, that's creepy sounding."

He shrugged. "I know, so you're apparently having a bad influence on me. What if? Depending on that answer we do have four."

My mouth dropped open. "Geez, you sound crazier than me, but the good news is, I think Mary might listen to you."

Chapter 14

You Found *What* in the Forest?

Sunday morning, at what felt like five A.M., I heard tapping on the post of our bunk bed. Then I heard "Psst."

"What?"

Mary peered over the bunk. "I lost my bracelet."

"In your *sleep*?"

"No, silly, I just realized it's missing, but it's not in the bed. I'm thinking it might have come loose while we were fishing. Y'know, with all that wrist flicking?"

"I'm sorry," I said, rolling over, hoping to doze back to my most amazing dream of winning an Olympic gold medal.

"Will you look for it with me?"

"Can we wait until sunrise?"

109

Mary giggled. "Oops, I'm sorry I woke you up so early. It's just that my parents gave it to me for my birthday, and I never take it off, even in the shower. We can wait until the guests are finished with breakfast. Do you want to go back to sleep?"

"Nope, that ship has sailed—I'll never get back to sleep now. Let's just get stuff rolling for breakfast. And to pay me back, while we're at the stream, you can show me where the land trust starts."

"Fair enough," agreed Mary. "We're serving ham biscuits today, so we'll keep a few back and take our food with us on the bikes."

That made getting up almost worth it, but it was still the kind of thing you only do for a friend. Or for a bracelet.

Breakfast seemed to take forever, but the guests had a good time. Grandma Gigi says that's what brings them back and makes them tell their friends. So we just kept pouring coffee and smiling. Gigi came on duty, chatted people up, handled the checkouts, and finally shooed us out the back door. Armed with biscuits and thermos bottles filled with milk, we pulled out the bikes and headed for the stream. It was sweatshirt and shorts weather, and as the sun rose over the mountains, we could tell that by noon it would feel like summer should. We parked the bikes where we fished on Friday, and carefully hunted, heads down, over every inch of where Mary had stood.

Unfortunately, all we saw were dirt and bushes. Mary was looking pretty teary-eyed, so I suggested widening our search to the area where she'd stood beside Alex and skipped her first stone. We both wore sunglasses, but hers were not polarized. Mine were, and soon I gave her the good news that I saw a piece of yellow metal fluttering in the stream just a few feet from the bank. Yup, not that far, but still twenty-four icy cold inches. That didn't stop my Girl Scout friend from tearing off her shoes and socks and plunging into the water, tree branch in hand. She poked the branch out in front of her, and said, "Guide me in."

My fancy sunglasses did their job, and a few seconds later, she was reunited with her treasure and warming up on the log bridge. "Wow, good work, roomie. Thanks so much."

"We were lucky some trout hadn't eaten it." As soon as her feet looked dry, I handed over her shoes and socks. "Now, can you get us to the red trail or do we have to go back to the inn and start over?"

She reached into one of the pockets of her cargo shorts, pulled out a compass, and grinned. "No need to go back, we can shortcut with this."

I shook my head and smiled. "I think you're the only person I know who owns a compass. *And* uses it!"

"I've learned some cool stuff in Scouts. Just wished I liked the uniforms better." Mary got up and pointed. "Here we go." She took off on what might be called a sub-path, which looked like it had been walked on but not groomed for bikes like the main trails.

"So," I said, "we saw Mr. Adams back here, and he was cutting through to the land trust. That part of the forest doesn't belong to Gigi?"

Mary shook her head, and said, "Nope. I think she owns sixteen acres, and that thing is more like forty. It's owned by heirs of some race car driver and will probably never be built on, so it's kind of like Gram gets the use of two forests."

"Cool," I said, "so then I guess it's okay Mr. Adams just charges around in here when he wants."

"Are we near where you guys saw him going?"

"Yeah, it was this direction, then he sort of veered that way," I pointed.

She ducked under a low-hanging branch, and said, "That's toward their land, but if he had permission, he's good to go."

"Okay," I said, shoving my bike along. "Then I'll stop going on and on about him, even though he said he was tracking a bird that doesn't belong in the mountains."

"And you know this how?"

We joined up with the other trail and looped back in the direction of the inn. I could see how we'd just made sort of a huge circle, and compass or not, I could find my way back here again. "Um, *my* grandma is a lifetime Audubon member in Virginia, and drilled nature stuff into me since I was tiny. I know way more about birds and butterflies than anybody should."

"Fair enough," said Mary, pointing us toward home. "Want to race?"

"Sure." I took off, leaving her in the dust. I flew along the trail, pedaling hard, until I saw something that made me skid to a stop, sending leaves and dirt flying. I yelled, "Mary, hold up." Just as the trail took a sharp dip, I saw an expanse of white metal over the edge. "Do you see that?"

Mary looked where I was pointing. "The white thing? What is it?"

I shrugged. "I think it's a car roof."

She leaned her bike against a huge oak tree and peered into the woods. "Gol, it's an SUV."

"I'll be right back." I slid down the bank and felt the vehicle's hood. "It's cold, so it must have been here awhile." The driver's side door was standing open, so I pushed it a little farther with my foot. "I don't see anybody." I did see a lot of typical junk that ends up strewn around in cars. There were some plastic drink cups and receipts, one from a factory in Georgia, one from a sandwich shop in Tampa. A couple brown pill bottles, like from when you're sick.

"What are you doing?" asked Mary. "Don't get too close to it. Sometimes cars catch on fire after wrecks."

"You weren't listening," I said. "The hood is cool, like it didn't just happen in the last hour. And I was looking at the stuff people leave behind."

"No suitcases burst open? That happened to us once. Stuff flew everywhere along the road."

"Nope, there's a little pile of powdery sand, like someone dumped it out of their shoe, and some reddish hardened piece of wood or mud, also like off a boot. And, it's weird, there are no broken windows, no blood, just some dust like this is an old car, but it's not, and sort of smells like oranges. Oh, yeah—it has New Jersey plates."

"Wow, too bad you don't have your notebook. You could be the reporter on scene." She leaned over the hill and pretended to hold a microphone. "Here is Emily Sanders, live from Winton, North Carolina, where a strange vehicle has mysteriously appeared. Film at eleven."

"Very funny," I muttered.

Mary giggled, "Well, it kind of is. Except, really you better get back up here. What if it tips over or something?"

Looking up from the vehicle, I could see its track through the woods. Broken branches and snapped saplings showed where the SUV had exited the Blue Ridge Parkway and tumbled through to here.

I shrugged, remembering what a worrier Mary was. And actually, she might be right; this thing was tilted at a steep angle. I climbed back up toward the trail.

Mary pulled her phone from a pocket, and said, "I'm never sure about reception out here, but let me try. Hey, Gram, we found my bracelet. Yeah, I know, it was amazing. Anyway, we were riding the trails, and we discovered a car wreck. There are some big dents, but no broken windows, and we're not sure if anyone's hurt, because nobody's here. The vehicle looks like it's been sitting awhile at the bottom of the ravine near the Parkway. Yes, right there at Pickle Run, but I don't know the mile marker. Is that enough info?" She listened, nodded and clicked off. "Okay, she's calling the sheriff's office and said we should hang out here for a few minutes until they tell her what to do."

I got to the top and brushed the sticky burrs from my socks. "Can I borrow your phone?"

Mary stared at me. "You're not going back down there."

"Yeah, I am. Unless you want to go snap a few shots."

She did the eye-roll at me, and said, "Does it look tippy?"

I shook my head. "No, and trust me, I do not want to be crushed. I just want to take some pictures."

She gave me the phone, and I slid back down the bank. Careful not to touch the door, I reached in and took shots of everything in the vehicle, including some brochures and other stuff that said, "Perry's Painting—Venice, Florida." Then something caught my eye. Sticking up out of the door pocket on the driver's side was a map that had an area of Winton circled and something scribbled in the margin. That something read "B. Den." Wow, maybe these were guests on their way to the inn. But if so, where were they?

"Hey, Mary."

"Yes, are you okay?"

"Stop fretting," I said, taking a shot of the map. "Did we have any guests that didn't show up last night?"

"I'm not sure, why?"

"I'll tell you in a minute." I pulled from my pocket the plastic bag that had once held my breakfast, and shook out the remaining crumbs. Then I squatted beside the SUV and scooped a sample from the pile of sand on the ground, careful to snag all the stray particles around it. I did the same thing in the other bag I had carried raisins in—this time getting a sample from the funny little pile on the other side of the SUV. I took a shot of the license plate, and was feeling like I could be on one of those forensic TV shows when the phone rang. I started up the bank, and answered it right as I got to the top. "Hi, Ms. Gigi, here's Mary."

"Okay, we're about a mile down the Red Trail. How long should we wait?"

We stared at each other while Gigi instructed us. Mary hung up and said, "Typical weekend at the peak of tourist season. The little sheriff's department up here is swamped. With no apparently injured people and no fire, they'll get out here when they can. They said not to touch anything. Did you?"

"Nope, but it was very tempting. You'll understand why when you see the photo stream. What about the open door?"

"I think a wrecker's on the way, so the deputy just told Gram we should vacate the area. She wanted us back anyway cuz a few guests have arrived, and she wants to take a quick nap before the rest come."

"Is she napping a lot lately?"

Mary nodded. "Maybe a little more, but I think she's worried about finances. All these new guests should help."

"True," I said, "so let's be good little kiddies, do what the deputy said, and vacate. I'm taking the lead again, so see ya!"

After we answered Gigi's questions about the wrecked SUV the best we could, Mary and I plunked ourselves down in the office. As we scrolled through the photos, she stopped at the one that said "Perry's Painting." "Should we call them to see if anyone is missing?"

"Oh, good idea."

Mary eyed the number, grabbed the desk phone and dialed. She shook her head and held the receiver so I could hear "This number is no longer in service."

"Google search?"

She nodded. "While I do that, do you think we should call the hospital?"

"Oh, like the emergency room? Hmm, another good idea." I glanced up on the chart of local phone listings on the wall, and dialed the hospital. When I got through to a person, I explained who I was, and what we were trying to find out. She transferred me to the emergency room operator, and I said all the same stuff again. "No crash victims? Yes, we reported it to the Sheriff's Department. Yes, ma'am." I gave her the number for Baird's Den and she repeated it back to me. "That's correct, and the switchboard is on all night. It might go to voicemail, but that's okay. Thank you."

As soon as I finished, Mary motioned me to look at the computer screen in front of her. She found a couple websites for Perry's in Venice, but one was for a marine supplier, and the painting one was "under construction." "That can mean the site actually is under construction."

"Or," I said, "the company has gone out of business. And, my personal favorite, this is a fake website."

Mary sighed. "So, what do we have?"

I shrugged. "Well, no car wreck victims listed at the hospital. At least none the lady would tell me about. She did say they'd call if there was any news. Now, what?"

"I don't know. I'm gonna make a PB&J and sit here in case any guests arrive." She looked at me. "Oops, let's check the book for last night."

I nodded. "Good idea. What's the note taped to the computer screen?"

"Gram must have forgotten to tell us. Moss's guys were delayed. Their car overheated."

"Funny, when you're up here and wearing a sweatshirt, you forget how hot it is off the mountain. Let's check the book."

We peered at the guest register until both of our stomachs roared with hunger sounds. "Well, if anyone in that car was coming here, they would have to be considered guests without a reservation?"

Mary considered my question, and then snapped her fingers. "Unless it's those Whidden folks. Gram had a question mark by their names, and they didn't guarantee late arrival. I'll call the deputy and give him their contact info."

I nodded and headed for the kitchen. Weird, thinking about people possibly wandering in the woods. Maybe they'd been kidnapped or eaten by bears? Okay, I can't possibly mention either of those things to Mary. But I might leave an extra night-light on, just in case.

Chapter 15

Uh-oh . . .

For early in the week, Baird's Den was hopping. This was probably because of several patrol cars, a wrecker, and an ambulance, which we all knew wasn't necessary, but apparently it's a precaution in the event injured people are found. An officer who frankly looked about a year older than me was in charge, since Sheriff Conyers was on vacation. This seemed like Officer Bennett's first rodeo. Every time he told us something, and we asked a question, he would say, "Oh, good idea." It got to be kind of funny, but we couldn't laugh, because some of the info was disturbing, especially to Grandma Gigi.

We had seven guests, all of whom were due to check out this morning right after breakfast. While Mary took care of that, I answered the phone, and Gigi sat in the kitchen with her hands clenched together as if she was trying to force herself to remain calm. Finally, there was a brief break, and we stood in the doorway, listening to the officer. "Okay, ma'am, this is where we stand. As you know, a vehicle with New Jersey plates ran off the Parkway and ended up in your woods. The vehicle, a late model Ford SUV, sustained a good bit of damage, but oddly no windows were shattered and only one air bag inflated. It appears there were two or more people in the vehicle, but there were only partial footprints, and they look to have been scuffed in a bit, like they were trying to disguise or cover them up."

Gigi asked, "Why would they want to do that?"

The officer pointed at her. "That was my thought exactly; why? Perhaps that would be due to what they were transporting."

"Transporting?" said Mary. "Like a tent or a cooler?"

He sighed and looked at Grandma Gigi. "Oh, I don't believe these folks were campers, ma'am. And, I'm afraid you folks steered me wrong, ma'am. That Whidden couple said they were not due here until next weekend."

Gigi sighed, and shook her head. "We must have had the date wrong on the reservation."

I flushed. "I bet that was my fault. It was only the second reservation I'd ever taken over the phone, and I obviously goofed it up. It was a rookie mistake. I'm so sorry."

Deputy Bennett peered over his black, plastic-framed glasses. "Yes, well, no matter. According to a map and several other items found in the vehicle, whoever was in the SUV definitely seemed to be heading your way or have some other tie to the inn."

Gigi looked puzzled. "Really? I wonder if they were looking for a place to stay."

"Perhaps," said the deputy, handing us each a form. "But until we get a bit further along, you may not want to be associated with this crowd."

"Why?" I asked.

"Am I free to speak in front of your staff?"

Gigi shrugged. "Of course."

"Well, ma'am, these folks were carrying several different types of controlled substances. So far, we've only found trace amounts, but when we get further into the side panels, and upholstery, we could find pounds of product."

"Speak English, deputy," grumbled Gigi. "Controlled, traces, product, do you mean drugs?"

"Yes, ma'am," said Deputy Bennett. "So, with the vehicle appearing to have some connection to your establishment, and now the presence of drugs, you can understand we're curious about your involvement."

"Involvement?" asked Gigi. "By that do you mean we made some phone calls and inquiries about the vehicle yesterday to see if anyone was missing or hurt? If so, my staff is guilty of that, but involvement in some criminal activity?"

"Or driving a drugmobile?" I blurted out. "We aren't old enough to need fishing permits, let alone a driver's license."

"That may be true, but I'm an officer of the court, just doing my job. For now, everyone here should be prepared to file a statement as to your whereabouts for the past twenty-four hours, and I would appreciate it if no one on staff leaves town. As a precaution, your staff and any vendors or service folks for the inn need to come by the department for fingerprinting. You have the forms they'll need to complete before arrival, and it's conveniently open seven days a week."

Gigi sighed. "We'll take care of it, Deputy Bennett. When will the vehicle be towed?"

"I believe the wrecker's on site, so they'll have it hooked up soon. There may be some tree work that will need to be done, and unless we can glean some information about ownership of the vehicle, you'll probably want to be in touch with your insurance company about the cleanup."

"Oh, my, this is just a nightmare. My rates are sure to go sky high. The department wouldn't help me with tree clearing and such?"

He thought for a moment. "It's not their habit to clean up private property from a car wreck. We certainly sweep the roadways and clear intersections, but not someone's yard. Sorry, ma'am. Any other questions?"

Looking grim, Gigi shook her head, exchanged business cards with him, and asked if he'd text her when the SUV was off the property. Mary escorted him to the door, and then went to give our boss a hug.

Chapter 16

What Do We Know?

When I got up to our room later, Mary was stretched out on her bunk staring at her phone screen. She sat up when I came in and said, "So, what do you think?"

"About what?" I asked, emptying my pockets and heading into the bathroom to brush my teeth.

"About being confined to Winton, being suspects in some sort of drug drama, and news flash, Gram is going to call your parents."

"Whoa," I said, standing in the bathroom doorway, "she can't send me home, we aren't allowed to leave."

Mary grinned. "Silly, she's not going to get rid of you, but she feels like your parents would want to know."

I held up a finger while I went to spit, rinsed my toothbrush, and sat on our tiny desk chair looking up at Mary. "My parents are pretty cool. I don't think they'll be upset or anything. Unless, of course, I was doing drugs, then they'd be freaked!"

Mary grinned. "True." She nodded to the junk I'd taken out of my pockets. "Is that stuff you filched from the crime scene?"

Redheads blush so stinkin' easily, it was pointless to try and look like who, me? "Well, *filched* is a pretty strong word, but I guess, technically that's what I did. There were these piles of dirt on either side of the vehicle. I told you they were kind of like someone dumped their shoes out."

"Oh, so they're not drugs?"

"I don't think so, but then, I don't know. Just in case, don't eat or even taste any of it." I got up and tossed her one, along with a piece of paper and pencil. "Let's see what we think this stuff is. What color is your pile?"

"Mostly white or just off-white, but with some tan flecks."

"Me, too, so let's write that down. Now, let's open the baggies and smell for a couple minutes." We did that, and I spoke first. "Um, it's a little bit like salad—vinegary? And, kind of a whiff of the beach, and maybe—"

"Oranges?" asked Mary. "Citrusy, to be sure. And, when you say beach, do you mean like sand? I'm dying to stick my fingers in here."

I nodded. "Okay, let's be official about this." We both wiped our hands with sanitizer stuff. The first pinch for me was smooth, and the second was bumpy. We exchanged similar "feel" reactions, which officially would probably be called "texture," but maybe not. It also felt soft and smooth, yet a bit grainy.

Mary held up her hand. "Go back a minute. As the resident baker, I smell maybe an ingredient, like sugar or flour. Since it doesn't smell sweet, and there's that beach/sand aroma, I'm thinkin' the other smell might be flour or maybe baking soda."

I nodded. "That's enough for tonight, but tomorrow let's see if there's any reaction to liquids. That might tell us a little more. Thanks for not laughing at me."

Mary smiled a sad little smile. "You are so serious about a bag of dirt it should be funny, but my Gram is scared and worried. I was just looking at the photos you took. Tomorrow, let's load them on the computer so we have a bigger image. Let's check anything we've got to see if something might give us a clue who was in that SUV." She zipped the bag shut, and then tossed it in the air. As I caught it, she said, "I say we keep pokin' around."

"Okay." I dropped both bags on the little dresser. I noticed a clunk sound from one of them, but just then my computer binged. "Oops, a mom-Skype, gotta run." No lack of news from my end, but the thing was, would I tell her all of it? Probably. She was a big girl, but would she remember I was too?

Chapter 17

What's Next?

The next morning, Gigi stopped me on the way back in from my run. "How does the trail look?"

I grinned. "Mary told you where I was?"

Gigi smiled back. "I was young once, missy, and curious. So?"

"Actually, it looks pretty good for being mangled by a gigantic wrecker, gobs of police people, and a news truck. Were you actually on the news?"

Gigi shook her head. "Thankfully, just a brief mention that a wreck happened 'in the vicinity of Baird's Den, and the investigation as to the whereabouts of the occupants of the vehicle is ongoing'."

"Well, lots of limbs are down, but the actual trail is passable on foot. It'll need raking and stuff like that."

Gigi guided me into the kitchen where I got some water and she fixed a cup of tea. "Alex was by earlier gathering up tools to start work down there. You must have just missed each other. The past few days have been very distracting, but we've got some international guests coming later this week, and I want us to wow them." She spooned some cinnamon sugar mixture into her tea, and stirred quietly. "So you, Mary, and I are going to be nose to the grindstone until this place gleams from every nook and cranny. Until then, there's no time for extracurriculars. Also, I need to call your parents and fill them in."

I nodded, feeling a little like my hand had been slapped, but knowing this nice lady was also my boss. "Mom Skyped last night, and I filled her in. She didn't freak out, but like you, she's concerned. I told her you might call."

"Great," said Gigi, looking at the doorway. "Ah, here's Mary. First, you two won't need to get fingerprinted. Sheriff Conyers left a phone message overnight. He'll probably speak to you both when he gets back, but no prints for now. I'm getting mine done in a little while. The guys from Mountain Artisans dragged in late last night. Their bad luck with vehicles continues. Something was goofed up with the lights on the store van, so they fussed around with it out back until the wee hours. They've already left for the shop.

"Lyle's back to start on some additional railings for the inn, so he'll be all over the place. If there's any need for the tree-felling chainsaw, Lyle will help Alex. Em, you're cleaning the second floor and sweeping the porches. Mary, when you're finished in the kitchen, dust the parlor and the dining room. One of us will help you as we can. We've got an anniversary couple staying here tonight, and Mr. Blanton's back. Busy day, my chickens!"

I grabbed milk, a banana, and a trail bar. The dining room guests had a spinach omelet casserole, which was probably delish, but green in the morning was a toughie for me, and I didn't feel like a sit-down breakfast. It was gorgeous outside, so I opened all the guest room windows and got started. I nodded to Mr. Holton as he headed to the attic, and noticed Gigi driving her cute little hatchback toward town. I had finished a couple of rooms when I detected a whiff of something drifting in the window. I sniffed, and thought hmm; maybe Mary had fixed a peanut butter bagel and toasted it too long. I shrugged and went on down the hall. It wasn't long, though, before she came running up the stairs. "Do you smell something?"

I nodded and said, "Anything specific?

"Yeah, something burning."

"Oh, rats. I thought I imagined that. Come on."

We sprinted downstairs, checked the kitchen and office, and went out the front door, looking for any sign of smoke. There weren't any guests here, but Mr. Holton was upstairs. He raised one of the dormer windows and hollered, "You girls know where that smell is coming from?"

Mary shook her head, and said, "No sir, but it's not in the house or the woods."

I went around toward the kitchen and the back of the house. Then I saw it, and yelled, "Smoke's in the carriage house. I'll grab a hose." I took off, hearing Mr. Holton say he'd call it in.

Mary said, "I'll get the other hose. Meet you at the entrance."

I'd never messed with fire before, but I guessed it wasn't smart to just fling the doors open. I got my garden hose as close as comfortable to the building, and Mary did the same with hers. Then we sprayed the doors, which hissed when the water hit them. Smoke drifted out, but it wasn't coming in big billows, and I hoped that was a good thing. Soon Mr. Holton joined us and said to keep spraying while he tried to open a door. He had boots on and work gloves so he was better prepped than we were, both wearing flip-flops and all. He peered in toward the bike storage area and motioned us to come closer with the hoses. We sprayed the bikes and mowers. Wow, what would have happened if we hadn't been here? The gas cans for the mowers were right there.

Suddenly, the rig from the nearest volunteer fire department roared up, and we backed out of the way. In minutes, the fire seemed to be under control, so Mary called Gigi.

One of the firefighters came out of the structure pushing a bike in each hand. "These two are toast, but the others are fine. Good job, girls."

Another firefighter opened the carriage house doors wide to let in the fresh air and provide more light. Another one fiddled with the breaker box. Gigi's car roared up the driveway and slammed to a stop. "Please tell me everyone's safe."

We nodded, Mary gave her a hug, and pointed to the scorched bikes. "This is the worst of it."

Gigi put a hand over her chest. "We're so lucky you girls discovered it."

I tapped my nose. "We smelled it. You develop everyone's sense of smell up here, and it apparently works in lots of different ways."

"Indeed," said Gigi, patting my hand. Then, she strode closer to the carriage house, pacing and waiting for the firemen.

Soon, one of them emerged and tipped his hat at Gigi. "Ma'am."

She looked up at him. "Any idea what caused this?"

"Well, I thought in this old structure, the wiring would be at fault."

"No," declared Gigi, "I remember my husband had that all redone not too many years ago."

"He did?" The fireman gave her an odd look. "Let me show you something. This shouldn't happen to newer wiring. A couple wires somehow worked loose and shorted out."

Gigi's shoulders sagged, and I thought she was going to slide right to the ground. She sighed like someone who'd lost her best friend, and in a way, maybe she had. This big ol' inn had been something she could count on for years, and now it was like it kept failing her. Mr. Holton said, "Not to worry, Ms. Baird. We'll get it back good as new. As the kids say, no harm no foul."

The fireman nodded. "That's a good way to look at it. I'll have to note the wiring issue in my incident report, and the chief will inspect things in a few days to make sure everything is safe. I believe he'll suggest storing the gas cans farther away from the mowers. I see you have a new fire extinguisher, so he'll probably run a quick staff training then, too." He nodded at Mary and me. "Though I must say, these young folks were quick on their feet to grab the garden hoses. Nice work."

Mary and I hugged each other in relief. It was cool to be able to think fast and make decisions, but wow, if this is what being a grown-up is like, I'm not yet ready to sign on the dotted line.

Chapter 18

What If?

Before Mr. Holton left, he came by the office to speak to Gigi. She beeped me on the walkie-talkie and asked if I'd pop downstairs. Apparently, she'd asked Mary too, so we all crammed into the office.

"Gigi," he said, "I saw what the fireman meant, and re-attached the wires. If it doesn't pass the Chief's inspection, you'll have to call in an electrician."

Gigi sighed. "Thank you so much. I'm so glad you were here."

Mr. Holton grinned and tapped his cap.

She said, "Girls, remind me to fill Alex in when he comes up from the woods. Come on, you old coot, I'll walk you out." They left out the back door, Gigi toting her gardening basket, and Mr. Holton heading for his pickup truck. A few moments later the bells on the front door jingled, and we saw the Gilliams, the cute couple celebrating their

25th wedding anniversary. They'd been to Magic Mountain and had an armful of souvenirs. We said hello, and they asked Mary. "Did we hear there was a fire here while we were out?"

Mary nodded, and said, "Yes, there was a little electrical issue in the carriage house. So small we were able to put it out before the fire engine arrived."

Ms. Gilliam said, "I'm dreadfully frightened of anything to do with fire. We'll stay tonight, and see if I can relax. If not, we'll head on toward Asheville tomorrow."

"I understand," said Mary. "If you want to see the fireman's report, I'm sure Gram would show you. We're perfectly safe."

"Well, maybe so. You'd hope she wouldn't put her grandchild in danger."

We smiled, and as we watched them climb the stairs, I said, "Cancellations are not good."

Mary frowned and said, "No joke, but thankfully, the Mountain Artisan guys are regulars. They might be back by the end of the week."

"Great," I said. "Question: you've been here before in the summer, yes?"

"Sure, every year, but I usually only stay a week or two. Why?"

"Is it typical for bad stuff like fires and falls to happen?" I asked.

"Of course not, silly. Why?"

"I know you've been saying I'm imagining things, but could all of this really be just accidents? I think we have to look at all these disasters again as if someone was causing them."

"Seriously?" said Mary, shaking her head. "Why would they?"

"I don't know, but there are too many things for all of it to have been by chance."

Mary sat for a minute, and then said, "I still think you're over-reacting. Everybody loves my Grandma Gigi, and there's no way anyone would want to hurt her. Well, except for that stupid Deputy Bennett, who wants an easy answer to his case. So, let's do what we were already going to do, and analyze the stuff in the baggies."

"Okay," I said, reluctantly. I only agreed because our immediate need was to prove the SUV was not associated with Baird's Den or with Gigi. Then I planned to get Mary to look at all the summer's crazy events to see if there was any way they could be connected. Since Alex was on my side, I hoped we could change Mary's mind.

~

Later, we spread the SUV photos on the floor and set the little baggies off to the side. Then I left, saying I'd be right back. I returned with four clear juice glasses, salad tongs, a full water bottle, dishtowel, two spoons, and some stir sticks. "I'm not one hundred percent sure what this will show us, but it feels like something we should do. We're gonna see if a little scoop of this mixture will dissolve in water. I'm pretty sure in science class we had to stir for three minutes."

"Can we test for drugs with water?"

"Not specifically, but we can figure out some stuff. From what I remember, flour floats and is not water-soluble, but I looked up cocaine and it is, so that would show us something. Then, sand sinks, and is not water-soluble or I'm guessing there wouldn't be any beaches. But salt will dissolve, so if the grainy stuff dissolves, we'd possibly have some guesses about what was in the baggies. Ready?"

We worked for a few minutes, and pretty soon we each had a glass with a blob of whitish/tan stuff suspended in the water. And we each had a glass with material in the bottom that looked like the beach. Since nothing dissolved, it didn't look to be sugar, salt, or even drugs, particularly cocaine.

"Hmm, I read something about sometimes cocaine is cut with baking soda."

"Cut?" asked Mary.

"I think it means mixed. That would reduce the strength and make it look like there's more product so they can sell more. I'll be right back." I ran down to the kitchen, rummaged through the pantry, grabbed a saucer, and tore back upstairs.

Mary looked up as I got back to the room. "Vinegar?"

I nodded, gently wiggling the bottle. "Don't you remember when the sixth graders made volcanoes last year?"

"Kind of."

I dumped a tiny portion of powder from my baggie onto the saucer. "The active ingredient in those volcano things is baking soda. It will erupt, or in this small a quantity maybe fizz if you pour vinegar on it."

"Cool," said Mary, picking up the bottle. "I'll just do a couple drops first." And she did. Nothing happened. "Maybe it needs a little more?" This time she did half a capful. Just a still puddle.

I shook her baggie. She dumped the first try down the drain, and we started over with a clean, dry saucer. Her sample proved just as unbubbly, and definitely no fizzing.

So, the bags potentially contained sand and flour, but no baking soda. Mary waggled her bag a bit, and said, "Does yours have a brown thing in it?"

I shrugged. "They're not identical samples. Maybe I snagged a little pine cone."

Mary tilted the bag, reached in with the tongs and pulled out a roundish twig an inch or so long. She sniffed it and grinned. "Well, it's banged-up, but it kind of looks like a cinnamon stick."

"Hmm," I said. "That makes as much sense as the rest of this. We've got beach sand showing up in the mountains, and someone carrying flour in a vehicle on a weekend romp along the Parkway." I sighed. "Let's look at the photos."

Mary nodded and downloaded them from her phone to my laptop. We scrolled through, and I pointed out the photo I took of the papers for Perry's Painting.

"Right," Mary said, "but it was a dead-end."

"Well, not totally, because it *does* say Venice, Florida, so that might explain the sand in the bags."

She pointed at the one from a sandwich shop in Tampa. "That's in Florida too, so that makes Perry's seem more important if we could locate them." She opened the photo of the receipt from the Middleton Mill, somewhere in Georgia. It had item numbers and letters on it, but no description, so we figured it was for parts from a factory. Finally, she opened the one that had the Winton map. It was very quiet while she sat and stared at the words B. Den. "Okay, this is what you think the deputy used to tie the inn to a drug mobile?"

I shook my head. "It seems to be the only thing, but if this was a cop show, it looks 'purely circumstantial.' That guy seems like Deputy Dawg, anyway."

Mary smiled and said, "Oh, for sure. I wonder when the real sheriff gets back."

Just then, Gigi peeked in and said, "Sorry to interrupt, but the deputy called to say the vehicle was definitely a rental, and did I know anyone by the last name of Krieger. I told him no, and he said not even a guest? So, I did that search thing you set up for me, Mary, and no Kriegers, at least for the past three years, which is as long as we've been totally computerized. Then he said that this Krieger was deceased, but his name appeared on the rental paperwork. So, that's probably not a good thing, but of course, nothing I have any connection to. He thought Sheriff Conyers would be back by the weekend, and he still might want to look at our guest information."

"I'm sorry, Gram," said Mary, looking like a lost little girl.

"Thanks, sweetie," said Gigi, "but honestly, to me, this all is so silly and a waste of time. I'm trying to treat this as an interesting life experience. What are you two doing?"

"Actually, we've just been talking about the sheriff's department. And we're looking at some stuff Em picked up at the crash site."

"Picked up?" asked Gigi. "We were instructed not to touch anything."

"Yeah," I said, "I didn't touch the vehicle or anything inside it. This was a sample from on the ground outside of it. Guess I can always say, wow, I'm just a kid, I didn't understand."

Gigi tried to hide a smile. "Oh, I'm sure Deputy Bennett would love that."

Mary said, "Look at this thing we just noticed. It's a twig that smells like cinnamon."

Gigi eyes widened. "Well, what you've got there looks like what we use to make the cinnamon bears. Some cinnamon sticks are weirdly shaped and those we grind up. That looks like a piece of a nice straight one. Come on, I'll show you."

We followed her downstairs to one of the kitchen pantries. She reached inside and pulled out a big bundle of the cylindrical sticks. "These are the Cassia tree cinnamon sticks Evan imports for me. These have a stronger smell, deeper color, and thicker bark that won't break easily, so they're perfect for crafts. I have an arrangement with Mariella, and split each shipment with her. I grind up my portion for the cinnamon bears and leave the rest as sticks for all her projects. Thanks to Evan, I only pay what it costs him to get the shipment here, and like I told Em, Mariella and I swap sticks for labor. All this keeps my cost per bear down. This jar has the cinnamon for making the bears." It was full of dark brownish color powder. She scooted down a few feet to the other end of the pantry. "And this one's full of the sweeter, lighter kind we use for baking or cooking."

"Wow," I said, "they look very different. I just thought cinnamon was cinnamon. Who knew?"

"That's my Gram," said Mary, throwing her arm around Gigi. "Smartest lady I know."

Well, maybe, I thought. But, instead of separating Gigi from the SUV, this information had made her connection much closer.

Chapter 19

Fact, or Really
Bad Fiction?

Later that afternoon, Gigi was showing the garden to a guest, and Mary and I were catching up on emails in our room. I finished and was checking my notes from the Moss interview when I thought about something. I realized Mary had fallen asleep, so I slipped out of my lower bunk as silently as I could. I tried tiptoeing down to the office, but when I got back upstairs, it was obvious I hadn't been all that quiet.

Mary grumbled, "What are you doing?"

"I'm still thinking about Gigi, the accidents, and the SUV. I borrowed the two spare whiteboards from the office, and thought I'd just slide in the bathroom and noodle around some."

"Do you want some help?"

"Always, but I didn't want to bother you."

"Really?" said Mary, aiming her handy flashlight at me. "Like you always say, that ship has sailed. I couldn't go back to sleep now, so open the shades and get writing."

I propped one of the boards on the dresser, and started filling stuff in. As soon as I began, Mary said, "Where did you start?"

"Well, at the beginning. There has been something weird about this whole summer. Maybe by looking at all we know we can figure it out, and come up with who might be the cause. Then, maybe we can help Gigi."

"Okay... I'm not seein' it, but keep going."

So I did. Soon, the first board was full, and I started on the second one. After a few minutes of filling in details, we looked at what I had.

If the 'Accidents' at Baird's Den are Not Accidents, then Who Could Have Caused Them?

Steps

- Someone possibly loosened the inn's back porch step.
- Nails were loose at one end of the step and missing at the other end.
- Nails did not appear to show rust.

Septic Tank

- Someone possibly killed the bacteria in the inn's septic tank.
- There was a smell of chlorine or bleach in the upstairs of the inn.
- The toilets started flushing slowly.

(Steps)

- Nails looked like they could have possibly been removed with a hammer.
- Nails were found near each other under the step area.

Candidates: Gigi, Girls, Alex, Bird Guy

Guests: Clayton Shaw, Jamal Greene, Mr. Randall, Ms. Randall, Jay Blanton (he was hurt on step)

(Septic Tank)

- There was a stink by the lawn over the septic tank.
- The system required the bacteria be replaced.

Candidates: Gigi, Girls, Alex

Guests: Clayton Shaw, Jamal Greene, Ms. Midge, Ms. Beverly, Businesswoman, Chicago couple

Bees

- Someone possibly attracted bees to the inn's attic.
- There was an active hive in the attic.
- A container was found nailed between the studs.
- Container could have contained sugar water.
- Bees possibly were attracted or even moved to the attic.

Candidates: Gigi, Girls, Alex, Mr. Holton, Bird Guy

Guests: Clayton Shaw, Jamal Greene

Fire

- Someone possibly sabotaged the carriage house wiring.
- The wiring is relatively new.
- Upon inspection, it appears some wires could have been switched causing a short & a fire.

Candidates: Gigi, Girls, Alex, Mr. Holton

Guests: Clayton Shaw, Jamal Greene

"Hmm, now I get it," Mary said. "So, how did you come up with the candidates?"

"By looking at who was here during or before the time of each incident."

"Got it," said Mary. "But I'd say we could eliminate the guests, the Bird Guy, and maybe Mr. Holton. They don't appear to have been around for all the accidents."

"All right," I said, grudgingly. "But the bird guy—"

"Don't go there. If we need to, we'll add him back in," said Mary. "Why do you have Alex with the fire?"

"Well, he was here shooting baskets and in the vicinity right before."

Mary nodded. "I remember that now. But you were with him the whole time, yes?"

"Actually, that's true," I said, thinking for a moment. "But he was *in* the carriage house early the morning of the fire."

"Really?" asked Mary, frowning.

"Yup, I didn't see him, but according to Gigi, he was getting tools for the wreck cleanup. Sorry, kiddo, he stays there for now. However, we could probably cross him off the bee incident. I mean, when he comes here, he's either in the kitchen, the office or outside, never the attic. I guess he could have had an accomplice, but that didn't work out so well as he was the one who got stung."

"Accomplice? Seriously, your mind never stops spinning. Take him off the bees, and now he's obviously off the 'all accident' list."

I lined through his name under 'Bees'. "Anything else?"

Mary pointed at the board. "Why is Gram a candidate? This place is her pride and joy."

I bit my lip, and was quiet for a long moment. "Don't take this wrong, but it's pretty obvious she's having some money trouble, especially with all the extra expenses. I'm not saying *I* do, but someone could suspect her as doing these things hoping to collect insurance money."

Mary had been sitting up in her bunk, but now sort of collapsed against the wall. "Are you kidding me? I never thought of that."

"I hadn't wanted to, but now you see why I think we should keep plugging away."

"I do," agreed Mary. "But look at our list. After all our snooping and including anything we can call evidence, we still only have a list of people we know fairly well, and in some cases, very well." She sighed.

I hated to make my friends sad. In desperation, I just let out what had been rolling around in my head. "Yeah, what we have does seem kind of lame. But what if someone on the list is not who we think they are or there's someone who should be on the list we've overlooked?"

"Wow, that's not lame, it's scary."

"I know, and it's starting to sound crazy."

"Except you're doing this for Gram, and crazy or not, I'm glad you are."

"Okay, then we'll keep going."

Mary yawned, and then pointed at the board. "I know we only took Alex off one thing, but what about running this by him?"

I thought a moment, remembering how we worked together analyzing the nails. He was smart, and it would be interesting to see his reaction to all this. Plus, he took one for the cause with that bee sting. "I think 'yes'."

"Hand me my phone, please." She leaned over the dresser, snapped a photo of the chart, and emailed it to him. "I said *Curious?*

Good, cuz we need your brain. Come by tonight, we'll explain." She giggled, and yawned again. "Great, I just sent a rhyming text. I'll wait right here for a reply. Until then, I choose sleep."

Chapter 20

Making Sense

It turned out to be a good night for whiteboarding, as by the time Alex arrived after basketball practice, Gigi had gone to bed. I realized we hadn't seen Alex since before the SUV landed in the woods. I was taking a load of trash to the dumpster and nearly mowed him down with the bags. "Hi, guy. Let me heave this in. Run into any bees tonight?"

"Nope, apparently they're asleep. How is it in the drug world?"

"So funny, but not for Ms. Gigi. We had a little fire in the carriage house yesterday, so it's kind of been like, what's next?"

"Yeah, I heard," he said, following me back to the inn. "I need to mow here tomorrow, so I wanted to check the mowers, and they seem okay. But about the other, I don't know what to say, except who would seriously suspect our boss of drug trafficking?"

I shrugged. "Honestly? I think a cop who's happy with the easy answer so he can look good to *his* boss. It doesn't sound like he's even checking any other possibilities.

And now the inspector is coming back, so we don't know what that means."

"Sorry to hear that," Alex said. "So what's the story about that goofy text?"

As we entered the kitchen, I said, "Yeah, we're almost ready. I hear Mary coming, so have a seat and I'll grab the cookie jar."

"I'll take a banana too," he said, pointing to the fruit bowl.

Mary stepped into the kitchen with the whiteboards, putting both on the counter leaning against the upper cabinets.

"Okay," I said, tapping the board, and then pointing to Alex. "I couldn't stop thinking about what's gone on since I got here, and wrote it all down. We've been looking at it and wanted to see what you think. Starting at the top, you and I examined the nails from the step and found stuff that didn't look right. Then, I added all the other bad events with supporting info. Finally, after the things you told me about Gigi's fall, I added *it* to our 'not accidents' list."

If the 'Accidents' at Baird's Den are Not Accidents, then Who Could Have Caused Them?

Steps

- Someone possibly loosened the inn's back porch step.

Septic Tank

- Someone possibly killed the bacteria in the inn's septic tank.

(Steps)

- Nails were loose at one end of the step and missing at the other end.
- Nails did not appear to show rust.
- Nails looked like they could have possibly been removed with a hammer.
- Nails were found near each other under the step area.

Candidates: Gigi, Girls, Alex, Bird Guy

Guests: Clayton Shaw, Jamal Greene, Jay Blanton, Mr. Randall, Mrs. Randall

(Septic Tank)

- There was a smell of chlorine or bleach in the upstairs of the inn.
- The toilets started flushing slowly.
- There was a stink by the lawn over the septic tank.
- The system required the bacteria be replaced.

Candidates: Gigi, Girls, Alex

Guests: Clayton Shaw, Jamal Greene, Ms. Midge, Ms. Beverly, Businesswoman, Chicago couple

Bees

- Someone possibly attracted bees to the inn's attic.
- There was an active hive in the attic.
- A container was found nailed between the studs.
- Container could have contained sugar water.
- Bees possibly were attracted or even moved to the attic.

Fire

- Someone possibly sabotaged the carriage house wiring.
- The wiring is relatively new.
- Upon inspection, it appears some wires could have been switched causing a short & a fire.

Candidates: Gigi, Girls, Alex, Bird Guy, Mr. Holton

Guests: Clayton Shaw, Jamal Greene

Candidates: Gigi, Girls, Alex, Mr. Holton

Guests: Clayton Shaw, Jamal Greene, Mr. & Mrs. Gilliam

Gigi's Fall

- Someone possibly tampered w/ basement steps light bulb
Candidates: Gigi, Alex, Mr. and Mrs. Beck

"You said *our* list?" asked Alex.

Mary took a deep breath. "Em's pretty much convinced me to go with her instinct and try to see if any of this would help Gram. If these events were not accidents, then who caused them? The candidates are people who were here before or during the event."

Alex pointed at the chart. "Mary, the light bulb in the basement either loosened itself through heating up and cooling off which caused the base of it to expand and contract. Or, someone loosened the bulb so the stairs would be dark. I can go into more detail if you need it, but truly either one is possible."

I nodded. "Right, and unfortunately it's the same thing for everything on this board. It's all based on how you look at it. Mary and I have been through this before. We learned that being suspicious is one thing, but you can't make accusations without proof."

"Hmm," said Alex, as he studied the board. "Does this mean I'm a suspect in four of these deals?"

I grinned. "Well, you were in all five, but we gave you a pass on the bees. So, either you had an accomplice or we can let you off the hook as being the cause of all this. We pretty much decided to let you off."

"Gee, thanks," he said, shaking his head.

Mary tapped him on the brim of his hat. "Looking at the candidates we identified but didn't eliminate, Emily made a good point. Since we know everyone but they don't strike us as crooks, maybe there's somebody we've missed *or* we don't know these folks as well as we thought."

"And because Gigi's problems continue to pop up, we've got to look at another issue," I said, writing on the bottom of the second whiteboard. "What about the stupid SUV?"

Mary put my laptop and the baggies on the table in front of Alex. Opening one of the bags, she said, "These are samples Em collected from beside the SUV the day we found it. We've done some testing of the stuff, and it appears to be sand and either flour or baking soda. Em also took photos of things inside the vehicle, and here they are." Mary scrolled through them. "The vehicle was a rental, but the name on the agreement belongs to a dead guy. It had Jersey plates, but might have been in Florida recently or connected to Florida. The last things are from Perry's Painting, Venice Florida, receipts from Tampa and Georgia, and some sand. Supposedly, there were drugs found, but Em didn't see anything like that. You saw the map with "B. Den" written on it, and that's the only thing the sheriff has to tie the vehicle to Gram."

I broke off a piece of cookie and ate it in one bite. Crime fighters must develop more cookie resistance the older they get or they would all be really fat. "Well, there's one more thing that might come into play." I reached in to the open baggie with the salad tongs, pulled out a little chunk of cinnamon, and put it on a napkin.

Mary said, "We're trying not to touch it, but this looks a lot like the kind of cinnamon sticks Gram buys for the bears and gives to your mom for her crafts."

Looking as grim as I felt, I said, "Technically, if the sheriff sees this, it could tie the SUV even more to Gigi, and maybe even to your mom."

"Ouch," said Alex. "I want to save my mom from your deputy, of course, but there actually might be someone else to consider." He pulled his phone out, scrolled through something on the screen, then held it up. "See the cinnamon sticks Mom used on this Christmas in July tree?"

I looked at the photo and then turned it toward Mary. "His mom is amazing."

"Yeah," agreed Alex, "she is, and so is Gigi. But as far as the cinnamon goes, they're the end users."

"Huh?" Mary said.

Instantly, I realized his point. "Oh, he's a smart one." I clapped my hands. "Tell her."

"Mom and Ms. Gigi *use* the cinnamon but it's *Mr. Moss* who imports it."

"Wow," said Mary, "you're right. But why would our Mr. Moss be involved with that SUV? And drugs? That's bizarre."

"Maybe," I said, "but there's a lot we don't know about him. Remember, he lets no one in the back of his store, and we've all wondered how he has such a fantastic business selling homemade crafts, when other shops here have closed. Hey, if I can imagine Mr. Blanton as a ruthless businessman with enemies, it's no big deal for me to see Mr. Moss being into drugs."

"Oh, that's just awful," said Mary, looking like she'd lost her best friend.

"Mary, I'm not saying he's a druggie himself. But he's a businessman, and there's lot of money in the drug world. Don't freak out yet, this is all still 'what if.'"

"It's wacko sounding," grumbled Mary.

Alex looked at her, then said, "Maybe not. Forget the drugs for a minute and concentrate on the SUV." He pointed to the laptop. "Can you go back to the receipts?"

Mary did, and when she got to the one from Georgia, he tapped the table. "That's it. Don't y'all recognize that?"

I looked at Mary and shrugged. "Should we?"

He said, "You two wrote the hangtags for the baking kits. This is the place they get the muffin mixes and the flour."

"We're idiots," I said. "Of course it is. The receipt didn't have the drawing of the mill on it, and it just had quantity, unit numbers, and prices, so we thought it was an order for parts for something. It didn't make any sense, and we actually didn't even Google the thing. But wait. You can buy flour at Winn-Dixie."

"Not this," said Alex. "Moss orders it in special. It's not sold in stores, which seems crazy to me, since it's pretty popular. They were on a waiting list for a month."

"Well," said Mary, "baker girl here knows we don't have any of this stuff in the house. So, that would skew this toward Moss more than Gram. But Mr. Moss has that red sports car and a store van, so why would he need an SUV?"

I actually had no answer for that immediately, so I sat quietly thinking and trying not to eat the rest of my cookie. "He wouldn't need to be the driver to be connected to it, right?"

Alex said, "True."

Mary snapped her fingers. "I'll be right back." And, in what seemed like an instant, she dashed back in waving a note. "I saved this in the book so we wouldn't bill Mountain Artisans for this night."

"Which night?" asked Alex.

"The one before the morning we found the SUV," said Mary. "The guys were delayed getting here because they told us their vehicle overheated."

"I remember that," I said. "We figured Mr. Moss went to get them like down in Charlotte or something because when we finally saw them, they were driving the store van."

Mary almost jumped up and down. "But if they were down there, and they always drive rentals, why not just get another vehicle?"

"Yeah," said Alex, "the only reason for *Mr. Moss* to pick them up would be if they needed a ride after wrecking the SUV."

"Wow," I said, "I've been a bad influence on you two. But it's beautiful. In theory, we've just connected Mr. Moss and his two guys to this SUV."

Alex and I high-fived, and then I noticed Mary had not joined in. She was staring at the other whiteboard. I asked, "What's up?"

"Well, I really do feel like I've crossed over to the dark side," said Mary, "but Jamal and Mr. Shaw are on this list in every spot."

"Except the fall," said Alex, pointing at it.

Mary scrunched her face, held up one finger, and headed to the office. I tapped my feet wondering which way this would go. Minutes later she was back with the guest book and other papers. "According to some doctor's notes the fall happened early in May, and they were here twice in April and three times in May."

I picked up the marker and added Jamal Greene and Clayton Shaw under Gigi's Fall.

Mary looked back and forth at us. "Oh, my. Our guys would do that on purpose? That's so mean."

Alex nodded, and said, "It is mean, but it possibly fits your idea of not knowing these folks the way you thought you did."

"And what we already knew about them," I said, "actually makes it worse. Whoever did these things would need to be handy and have access to tools. They do. The fire? I'm pretty sure they were here. Seemed like Gigi said something was wrong with the store van, and they'd been working out back late into the night right before it happened. Mary and I have talked about the septic tank/bleach/chlorine thing with them and the Target bags."

"Sounds like we might be onto something," said Alex.

"Maybe," said Mary, "but what?"

I answered with a question. "If they were in the SUV, why would these two be there?"

"Because they were working?" replied Mary.

"And they work for?" I asked.

"Mr. Moss," said Mary, looking at me like I'd lost my mind.

"Or, they work for Mr. Moss by day, and have a little business on the side running drugs?" asked Alex.

"Either scenario is possible," I said. "But, let's get back to the whiteboard. With their names potentially connected with every event, if they caused the events, why would they?"

"Because they were working," said Mary

"For who?" asked Alex.

Looking super confused, Mary answered, "Mr. Moss."

Alex smiled. "And, now you might have discovered the missing person for the list."

"But why would Moss want to hurt Gram like that?" asked Mary.

"I don't think he does, Mary," I said, "but she might just be the casualty along the way of him getting the Baird's Den property. You told me lots of folks have wanted it for condos, and in my interview, he described the land around here as a gold mine."

Alex nodded. "He's told mom the shop's run out of room and needs more space."

Looking forlorn, Mary said, "He always acts so concerned Gram's overdoing it." She stood quietly for a moment. "But, he's also definitely planted that idea the inn might be too much for her. That creep. I'm ready to talk to the sheriff."

Alex said, "You two know how much Mr. Moss is liked here, right? The sheriff might laugh us out of the station if we accuse him of any of this stuff with just that piece of cinnamon."

"Then we need more evidence," said Mary. "I think we should go to the shop."

"Me too," I murmured. "I wish we could get into that back room."

We all nodded.

Alex looked at the kitchen clock, and said, "I must sound like a wuss, but I'm beat. But I'm in on your plan. You two go to the shop as late in the afternoon as possible, and I'll meet you there. Mary, take your phone and snap a photo of the baking kits and close-ups of the ornaments. There are cinnamon sticks all over the tree. I don't know what else we'll see, but it's worth going. Plus, you can grill my mom some. You won't have to talk much, just listen!"

"We can't *pin* the SUV on Moss, but possibly we can tighten the connection with some of this stuff," I said. "And maybe while I'm cleaning anyway, I should do a quick search of the Whistle Creek room where a certain two guys usually stay."

"Oh, Em, it's not a bad idea, but other people stay in that room, too. Maybe back when this happened we might have found something, but now? Not so much."

"Yeah, you're right. I had the perfect cover, I'd be looking for a prior guest's lost pearl earring. Think they'd notice if I busted into their car?"

"Right," Mary said, laughing, "and if you need me to, I'll distract them by doing backflips. Seriously, we've got to let this nice guy go home."

"Right," I said, feeling bad we'd kept him up so late. "I'm heading up, but take cookies for the road, Alex. Do you have lights on your bike?"

"Yes, mother," he said, patting me on the head. "Very safety-minded if only I can stay awake."

As I headed up the back stairs, I could hear them talking softly as Mary walked him to the front door. Aww, we got a helper, and maybe she was getting a boy!

Chapter 21

Eyes Wide Open

I made the coffee Wednesday morning, and went back up to tidy a couple of rooms. When I got back downstairs, I saw the Gilliams at the front counter with their suitcases. Uh-oh.

"Well," said Gigi, "I'm so sorry you were worried and didn't sleep well. The fire was just a few sparks from some wires in the carriage house. Everything's been corrected. I would be happy to have y'all stay tonight at no charge."

"No, thanks," said Ms. Gilliam. "We're all packed and have a nice place picked out to stay in Asheville. Thank you for a lovely time, and we'll check your website to see how things are going next time we're headed this way."

I couldn't see Ms. Gigi's face, but I was sure she'd be sad to lose these folks. We still had Mr. Blanton for tonight, and the Irish couple were due in tomorrow, so it wasn't super bleak, but close. Mary came quietly up behind me, and said, "I heard coming down the stairs. Rats."

"Yup, anything else going on?"

She looked puzzled. "I honestly don't know. I took a phone message from Melanie Williams' mom, and she wants Gram to call her back."

"I'm dusting books in the library, and then I'm headed to do some laps at the Y. We're still going to Mountain Artisans later, yes?"

"Sure. For now, I'll wait for Gram in the office."

Fifty dusted books later, I heard Gigi ask, "Where did you hear a rumor that Baird's Den was for sale?"

I realized I could hear Ms. Williams' voice, so Gigi must have the speaker on. I scooted to the office doorway.

"Well, I don't remember just where I was when I heard about it. Of course, you've been on the news, too, so that could be it."

"The news?"

"Well, yes, about that wreck and some rumors about drugs being found. Of course, I don't believe for a minute that you are involved with any of that. I just wanted you to know if you are interested in getting out of the lodging biz, I'd love the listing."

"If and when I ever decide to do that, Suzanne, I'd certainly keep you on my short list of realtors. However, that's not the case right now, and I still wonder how you made the jump from a wrecked vehicle on my property to the inn being up for sale."

"Hmm, let me think where I was." There was a long pause and a good bit of throat-clearing. "I don't think it was your granddaughter, but maybe Melanie and that Ortiz boy were talking. He's a cute one, but a bit young for her. I *do* have a need for a yard boy on some properties. Think he might be interested?"

Mary maturely stuck out her tongue, and I grinned, loving the drama.

Gigi said, "I'll give him your number, but we keep him pretty busy here. You were saying?"

"My word, it seems like there were several different folks at coffee the other morning. The new editor of the paper, Evan Moss, and a couple others, maybe even Reverend Samuels. I can't be sure just who actually proposed it."

"Well, Suzanne, when you remember that little detail, why don't you give me a jingle. I look forward to hearing from you. Bye." And Gigi clicked off. Good for her!

Gigi looked grim. "I wonder if our Irish guests will still show. It was going to be such fun having them here."

Mary said, "Of course they're coming. Remember, I talked to them yesterday, and really laid it on thick how incredible this place is."

"Well, you would, you're my granddaughter."

"Yes, ma'am, but they didn't know that!"

"Well, girls," said Gigi, "I appreciate your support and attitudes so much. Would you mind if I ducked out of here for a bit? I think I'll head to the spa for a massage treatment."

"Go crazy, ma'am," I said, "and have a pedi, too."

"You two are a riot," said Gigi. "But, I will stop by Becca Bakes and order some scones. Then, the Irish folks will have to show up, won't they?"

Gigi had just left when the phone rang again. We both reached for it. "Baird's Den, this is Mary."

"Yes, ma'am," said Mary, "she's right here, Ms. Blackstone. If it's okay, I'm putting you on speakerphone."

"Hi, it's Emily," I said. "Thanks for calling me back. We were just talking about the bees."

"Well, that plastic jug your carpenter found wasn't mine. I'm sorry I missed it when I was scoping out the area. You said it was very sticky and smelled sweet. I'd say someone at some time had tried to encourage a hive or move a hive there. As you might remember, I used something similar to capture yours. But you said it was a plastic jug, and I always use glass. Not sure why, but I'm a re-user type of gal. Also, my logo is on every piece of equipment, so that's another way to tell. Maybe someone once wanted bees *in* the attic, not out."

"Okay then, that's very helpful," I said.

"Well, it's still sort of a mystery, but I wanted you to know."

"Thanks for following up with us," said Mary. She clicked off and turned to me.

"The guys were here before the bee stung Alex, yes?"

She turned to the computer screen, tapped a few keys, and nodded. "Yes, remember they were working up—"

"In the attic! Yeah, that was when Jamal hurt his shoulder."

"Right." She scrolled down through dates, then poked the screen. "Then, about a week later, they were back and looking for a tool Mr. Shaw left somewhere."

"And that somewhere was probably the attic. We honestly don't know what they were doing, because they come across as so trustworthy. But an opportunity existed."

~

As of late in the afternoon, Gigi had no word from the couple from Ireland. However, since the lady was a landscape architect studying in the States for the summer, and touring through North Carolina on her way to speak at Biltmore House, we all felt pretty good about them still showing up tomorrow. Mary and I pedaled along toward town, talking about her growing almost an inch since school let out, and how sometimes it makes you sore to grow so fast. I would like it since swimmers are supposed to be lanky, and I'm basically just muscular, all in proportion, but not so long and lean. Mary is tiny but strong, and now that she's grown some, several people have approached her about soccer. "I heard from Sam again," giggled Mary. "He won't let up on me trying out for the Magic travel team."

"Bet he isn't hearing you when you say you've never played soccer."

"Nope, you know how he is, very one-tracked if it's about soccer."

I smiled thinking of Sam. We were good friends who thought we wanted to date each other last year. Neither of us felt a spark, so friends we would stay, which honestly made my life so much simpler.

We got to Mountain Artisans before we had Mary's sports future figured out, so I guess she'll have to remain a gymnast for a while longer. As we parked our bikes, we both noticed that the space where Mr. Moss normally parked his little red sports car was filled with a minivan from Pennsylvania, so we figured he was still over in Tennessee. We peeked at the giant fir tree filling the front window and tried to ignore it because we were there on a fact-finding mission. But as soon as we entered the shop, the evergreen smell hit me. Yes, I was in shorts and a T-shirt, but this shop smelled like Christmas. We waved at Ms. Ortiz's greeting and tried to focus on the reason for being there, our mystery.

"Psst," whispered Mary, "the baking kits are right here."

I picked one up and studied it. As I watched Mary snap photos of the kits, I wondered how we could have forgotten these had stone-ground flour in them that came from Middleton Mill. Guess we were focused on the cute dishtowels made by Alex's mom, and the cool spatterware pans, but still.

We headed toward the Christmas tree, and soon Ms. Ortiz hustled over, giving each of us a hug. "What do you think?"

I grinned and looked around. "It's magic. Who would believe it's the middle of summer? Was it fun?"

She smiled and then sighed. "Yes and no. I'm not too structured, so if something looks a little wonky, I'll just wing it and brush on another layer of glitter. Mr. Moss isn't so easily satisfied. He wants everything perfect. We sometimes butt heads, if you excuse my expression. I enjoy a day like this when I'm here on my own. We actually sell more stuff on my days."

"Good for you," I said, glancing at the windows where people peeked in and then entered as if they were pulled along by a magnet. "Anything special we should look for on the tree?"

"Yes," Ms. Ortiz said, "These ornaments are my babies. See the little nests, the miniature balsam pillows, and the toy bags filled with cinnamon sticks? Then there are cinnamon stick stars and bundles. Doesn't it all smell amazing?"

Mary and I giggled at how excited she was, and I said, "It's like smelling one of Mary's breakfasts at the inn, fried apples with all the cinnamon or coffee cake."

Ms. Ortiz said, "And I get to enjoy it all day long. Mary's *abuela*, Gigi, gives me the cinnamon sticks in exchange for making the bears. Then I have no cost in the materials and can make all the cinnamon joy you see here." Her face broke into a huge grin. "My baby boy!"

Alex had come in, and he made his way to us all gathered around the tree. "See, I told you. This is one amazing tree."

Just then, three people waved at Ms. Ortiz with things they wanted to purchase so Alex pointed out some of his mom's other creations to Mary. I had to use the bathroom, so I headed for the rear of the shop. The women's bathroom was a single, and definitely was decorated to impress. Even the soap was really neat, very citrus smelling, which probably appealed to all the Florida visitors who flocked here in the summer to get away from the heat. As I came out of the bathroom, Ms. Ortiz was waiting for me with one eye on the front counter. "I wanted to make sure you were okay."

"Oh, I just needed to use the restroom." I pointed to a sign that said "Keep out—No Admittance" and said, "This is the best old building, and I'm coming back tomorrow to take photos to go with an article I'm writing. It would be neat to get some shots of the brick—think he'd let me back there?"

Ms. Ortiz shook her head. "I wouldn't count on it. The only people allowed back there are Mr. Moss and his full-time workers. He said when he first opened the shop, he was too approachable, and customers wandered back there all day long. That door stays locked, and the key lives under the counter. We're only to use it if there's a fire."

Ms. Ortiz hustled off toward a new group of customers. I slid in beside Mary and Alex at the wind chimes. "Are you ever going to buy one of these?"

She nodded. "I am, right now."

"Finally," I said. "Just for fun, when we leave, let's spin around back."

"Okay," she said, "but I wanted to show you the library, not tour the dumpsters in the alley."

Alex leaned his head toward us both and spoke quietly. "On every cop show you ever see, forensic teams scour the trash cans."

We said our good-byes, grabbed our bikes and headed around back. We walked between two multistory brick buildings, and the heat from the day felt good. When we got to the dumpster area, I burst out laughing. "I thought the dumpster at the inn got crammed full, but this is way worse."

Mary nodded. "You know, some people come to Winton and go to the fudge shop. Not us!"

I grinned. "Yes, but those people aren't hunting for evidence to prove their suspicions are correct. Do y'all see anything here that could help us or is it just a bunch of cast-off junk?"

Mary scrunched her face in thought and peeked around. "Well, there's a ton of cardboard, but that's how their stuff comes. There are lots of labels in foreign languages, but he imports a bunch. Hmm." She was getting into the game now, and she stood on tiptoe to peer in further. "Hey, Em, we never caught up with anyone at Perry's Painting, did we?"

I put my hand on one hip. "Nope, why?"

"Then, again, maybe we did," said Mary, and she stuck a foot in one of the metal supports on the side of the dumpster. Up she went, stopping just short of toppling in. She reached over some pieces of wood and puffy packing material, and said, "Okay, you two. I take back everything I said about dumpsters. Em, catch!"

In seconds, I was holding a scraped-up, but still very readable magnetic sign, just the right size for the door of a certain SUV. I still didn't know who Perry was, but I was holding his sign!

Chapter 22

The Plan

I put the sign under my arm and headed toward my bike. "Come on, let's roll."

"You're stealing it?" asked Mary.

Alex said, "It was dumpster dived, not stolen. We're just lucky we came today, because the trash truck comes early tomorrow. Here, put a piece of packing foam over it, slide it in the bag with Mary's wind chime, and you're good to go."

I nodded, did what he said, and then looked at them. "Is this enough to take to the deputy sheriff?"

"It might be." Alex shrugged. "I don't know him very well, but my guess would be he'd shuffle his feet and say anybody could have heaved this into the dumpster. Also, why would it be Moss or his helpers? He owns this great business and does so much for the community. And, what would a sign prove if there really wasn't a Perry's Painting anyway?"

Mary said, "Yeah, I had mixed feelings about trying to pin something on Mr. Moss, but after Ms. Williams' call this morning, and this sign, I'm leaning more toward believing he's not what he seems."

"What call?" asked Alex.

I told him, "Melanie's mom is a realtor, but I'm sure you know that. Anyway, she said she'd heard Ms. Gigi might want to get out of the lodging biz, and while she just couldn't remember who said it, she heard it at coffee the other day."

"Huh?" Alex asked.

"Yeah," I said, "there are some folks who gather at the drugstore for coffee and chitchat." Mary nodded. "And guess who was there recently? Evan Moss."

"So, if Ms. Williams is right, maybe Mr. Moss really does want Gigi's property," Alex said, "and at a rock bottom price due to a series of unfortunate events. Well, I've seen how tough Moss can be, so even though he's nice, he could have a dark side. Mom works eighty hours a week sometimes, but he says she's an 'independent contractor' because she does the craft work from home. He pays her by the piece, not by the hour. He *says* it lets him pay her more since he saves on taxes and stuff. From her end, she gets no benefits like vacations, no medical insurance and no workman's comp. Sorry for the speech, but it's kind of cheesy, huh?"

"Definitely," said Mary. "This is hard for me, but what we need to do is forget we all have a relationship with him, and keep up the hunt for proof. That's the only way we'll find out if he's a good guy or a bad one."

"Agreed," I said, "but I'm leaning more toward bad guy, because good guys usually don't mind having their picture taken."

"Huh?" asked Alex, "what do you mean?"

"During my interview with him, he made a definite point about how he didn't want to be photographed, and I could shoot anything else, just not him."

Mary said, "That's sort of weird."

"No joke," I said.

Mary pointed to the back door of the shop. "What do you think is behind that door? Maybe a stock room and an office?"

"I don't know, but it's big," I said, "so he must have tons of stock. I've been here twice, and Melanie and Ms. Ortiz both said no one goes back there except Mr. Moss and his full-time staffers."

"A.k.a. your two regular guests," said Alex. "And another suspicious thing that could mean something but still proves nothing."

Mary nodded. "Well, we've got to split, because the library's closing and someone could come along and see us," she said. "What should we do?"

"I think we need get into the mysterious back room," said Alex, "but how do we get past the locked door?"

"Your mom came to check on me in the bathroom and ended up telling me the story of the door. There's a key to it that stays under the counter. So, we come back again late tomorrow. I'll jump around here and there for my article, take photos of the merchandise, the store, you two, Mr. Moss, oops, *not* him, and ask about the neat old brick in the back of the store. He'll either let us in, or not."

"And?" Mary asked.

"He won't let us, but I roam all over the shop. At some point, right near closing time, I have to pee, go into the ladies' room, use it, wash my hands, turn off the light, and lock the door. You two leave and move all three bikes to the rear of the shop. He'll close up, get in his little sports car, and take off. Then I can come out, get the key, and sneak into the forbidden back of the store."

Alex said, "Yeah, I got this. We'll be keeping an eye on when he leaves, and when he does, we'll bang on the back door, like five times. You hear it, come let us in this door. Then, we photograph anything that helps us prove he's after Gigi's property or that ties him to the drug mobile."

"Hmm, we'll have our phones," Mary said, "and Em will have her camera. Do we need anything else?"

"Water and money," Alex said.

"Say what?" I asked.

"We tell Ms. Gigi we're going to the movie in the park. It doesn't start until dusk, but that will give us all the time we need without her worrying."

"Good idea," said Mary. "If you think of something else, text."

We all stood staring at the back door of the shop. I wasn't sure what the others were thinking, but I was mostly thinking wow, we have a chance to find something to really help Ms. Gigi. We also had a chance of getting arrested for trespassing, but that wasn't very helpful, so I dismissed that idea immediately.

Chapter 23

A Slight Adjustment to Plan

The next day, the Irish guests, Mr. and Mrs. Gallagher, finally arrived. I'm not sure if it was the sparkly clean inn or the scones and teaberry tea, but they loved us. Gigi told us we could serve the bedtime snacks later than usual tonight, so we were good to go to the movies in the park. She asked if anyone else besides Alex would be joining us, and before I turned beet red from embarrassment, Mary said, "Not this time, Gram. Just we three."

Mary and I grabbed some water bottles and trail mix bars for later, and headed upstairs.

When we got to our room, I said, "I need the camera battery from the charger. I can't believe it, but I'm nervous."

Mary said, "Me too, but then I think of Gram, and just get mad."

"Hah, great idea. That'll keep me calm." I changed into jeans and T-shirt, and tied a hoodie around my waist. I first put on flip-flops, but then thought of the wet grass as night fell, and tugged on socks and sneakers.

Mary was dressed all in black, T-shirt, jeans, and strappy little sandals, and had a sky blue and purple scarf wrapped around her neck. I guess that was kind of like a sweatshirt, only way more fashionable. We both tucked little flashlights into our pockets, plus money, a Baird's Den card each with our name on it, and lip gloss. Well, actually I had a tissue, but when I saw Mary pop in lip gloss, I thought okay, probably time for me to think of stuff like this.

I did remember one thing and opened a drawer. Mary's parents had sent gifts to us when they got back from their cruise. Mine was a teeny bottle of French perfume, and Mary'd had to show me where to dab it, like on the inner part of my wrists and on my neck. We had cracked up that I didn't know much about perfume, but I'd promised to start learning. I still was having trouble figuring out how much a dab was, and sometimes overdid it. Like tonight apparently.

Mary waved her hand, "Phew! You did it again. Remember one droplet goes a long way."

I sighed, no doubt looking sheepish, and we were off.

We met Alex a few blocks from Front Street, conferred about some details of what to do first, took deep breaths, and aimed ourselves at Mountain Artisans. Weirdly, we met up with Jim Adams, the Audubon guy, as he left the shop. We hadn't seen him at Baird's Den in almost a week. Funny, even though he kept popping up around the inn and I still didn't believe his whole story, his timing didn't mesh with more than one or two of the incidents. Anyway, I guess he'd been looking for Alex's mom, and Moss set him straight about her schedule. It didn't sound like those two guys were best friends, but today, that was pretty low on my interest level.

As we entered the shop, Alex had an idea. "Just roll with me on this. I'm going down to the hardware store for a minute. Seeing all three of us at once might make it too obvious that we're a group. He's used to seeing you two together. I'll be back soon."

We went on in, and I waved my camera. "Hi, it's photo day. Are we good?"

Mr. Moss looked at the clock and said, "Sure thing. My new part-timer has a sick kid, and I haven't had a break all day. If you two can hold down the fort for like fifteen minutes, I need to make some phone calls."

"Where's Melanie?" I asked.

"Well, she had some sort of emergency come up."

Mary glanced our way and said, "Really? Is she okay?"

"I think there was a shopping trip to Charlotte involved." He shrugged and smiled. "It's hard to fire a volunteer."

I tried not to notice him reaching under the counter for the key, and said, "We'll be fine. Go make your phone calls."

"Great, and if someone wants to buy something, just stall 'em a bit."

"No problem." I watched him disappear into the back, and just for fun, headed in that direction. I edged closer to the door, listening, but not hearing any conversation.

Mary cleared her throat.

I looked her way, only to see she was crooking her finger at me. Like a small child, I trudged to the front.

"Get away from that door," she said, shaking her head. "He'll be back out here soon. It could get ugly if you were standing there when he does. We sure don't want to tip him off that we suspect him, especially if we don't find enough evidence."

"You're good at this. I just need to make sure he puts the key back." I turned around, hoisted my camera and took several shots of the whole shop, then individual sections. I hoped these would be usable, as photography wasn't my strong suit. In most of my photographs, I chopped the tops of people's heads off, or their legs, stuff like that. But honestly, for an article in a local paper, they didn't have to be great. If the paper liked the article enough to buy it, they'd send their own photographer. I just needed to give them the idea of what was here. Mary perched on the stool at the far counter like she was a clerk, and pretty soon, I had her modeling with some of the citrus soap and lotions. Like me, she was super impressed by how good they smelled.

"I might buy one of these for our bathroom," said Mary. "Plus, I might concoct my science project from this crazy summer."

"You're not talking about school right now, are you?"

Mary giggled. "Nope, but I did run a quick search on smell. Apparently the citrus scent makes people more trusting. And there are studies that show it can influence people to donate more money for a cause, like a charity."

"Or buy more stuff at an upscale store?" I asked.

Just then, Mr. Moss came out from the back with coffee and an apple. He nodded to us, put the key back, and started eating. I snapped a few more shots of Mary holding different things, and then turned to the tree. Mary left the area and headed toward the bathroom. About that time, Alex came in, and Mr. Moss and I both greeted him. He shook Moss's hand, and then came over to me at the tree. I said, "Grab that log carrier and do something with it, please."

He did, and Mary came over posing as if she was hanging ornaments on the tree. Then Mary said she needed to run down to the drugstore before they closed. Next, a bunch of customers came in, so

Moss barely had time to have a swig of coffee before ringing up a number of items. Everyone left with at least one bag, and several came in for the last few pies. Alex suggested a few more shots, and I asked Moss if he minded if I tried some artsy type shots of the exposed brick and the windows with the Christmas quilts and stuffed animals made from the antique quilts.

Basically, he could have cared less what we were doing, and soon it was close to closing. Mary had come back, and I left to "get something from my bike bag," then slipped back in with some new customers. I stayed with these folks as they moved around the shop, and out of the corner of my eye, I saw Mary and Alex leave. I gulped and split off from my group toward the restrooms. I had a slight hiccup as several women were waiting to use the facilities, but I made sure to be last in line, and finally it was my turn. I locked the door, peed, flushed, washed my hands, and when I was finished with the noisy stuff, turned out the light.

Mr. Moss had flashed the store lights on and off about ten minutes ago, so as the lights began to switch off and stay off, I peeked at my glow-in-the-dark watch, and saw it was ten minutes past his normal closing time. I felt a little knot in my stomach and wondered how long I would have to wait in here. It suddenly occurred to me that Moss might check the restrooms for stray customers, but thankfully, he didn't. It seemed like hours, but actually was only about fifteen minutes before I heard five loud knocks from the back of the building. Showtime!

I slipped out of the bathroom as quietly as possible, and realized the sun hadn't set yet, so I could actually see pretty well. I grabbed the key and unlocked the mystery door. It stuck a bit, but finally swung wide. I propped it open and replaced the key so when we left out the back way, no one would know we'd been there. I worked my way across the warehouse area to the outside door. There was a little button lock to twist, another doorknob to twist, and poof, there were my partners in crime. "Get in here, quick!"

We sprinted around in a group, peeking in three separate doors. One was the office, one was an empty office, and one was a storage closet filled with mostly backup supplies of the crafts. Some of these were Ms. Ortiz's things; some were kind of tacky stuff that must have been imports from some of those foreign countries whose names we saw on the boxes in the dumpster. The rest of the back room was just that, a big room with two long worktables and a few chairs. There were sort of workstations set up with scissors, some tool that looked like something my mom planted tulip bulbs with in the fall, drills with boring bits, like to make holes, glue guns, staplers, markers, and a few small artists' brushes. I whispered, "Alex, your mom and her crafters work at their houses, yes?"

He nodded, and shrugged like, "What's the deal?"

Mary said, "There's nothing to take a picture of, unless you want me to look in his desk. We could check bank records, but that's probably going to need passwords."

I shook my head. "Nope, let's try the storage closet again."

We went in and stood quietly staring at the shelves. At the end of one, Mary lifted the lid on a plastic storage bin, tilting it toward us. It was full of cinnamon bears lined up in rows like they were waiting for something. From that point on, there was an object, like a floral arrangement on a shelf, then underneath it a good-sized box with an arrow pointing up to the object, so you would assume there were more of that object in the box. We all looked at each other, and then opened one box each. They weren't sealed, so the opening part went fast. The gasping part did not. Inside each box were baggies of what? Let's see—firmly packed whitish powder in some, pinkish powder in others, and blackish grassy-looking "herbs" in others. Mary's Google search on her phone said we could be looking at bags and bags of cocaine, heroin, and hashish. Scads of drugs, right here in Winton!

Even though we still had no idea how it all tied together, we finally awakened from our shock and started taking pictures of everything. Alex and Mary were stuffing their phones back into their pockets when we heard two car doors slam in the alley. We'd planned for a bunch of scenarios, none of which involved encountering any people. I started for the front door, but Mary whispered, "Metal gate." I nodded, remembering Mountain Artisans had one of those old-timey black expandable things slammed down in front of the wooden door.

We squatted down behind the multitude of boxes in front of us. I'm not sure what Mary and Alex did, but I dredged up a few prayers. One was answered immediately as it came to me we shouldn't stay where the "product" was stashed. "Come on."

We ran as noiselessly as possible to the empty office, hoping logic led us to the place nobody would think would be inhabited. We left the door ajar, just like we'd found it. There was no closet, or even a coatrack in here, but there was a desk, so we ducked behind it. And we waited, trying to breathe but not too much.

Chapter 24

This Stinks!

As we heard the sound of a key in the back door lock, Mary and I wiped our brows, like "Whew," glad we'd re-locked that door. Mr. Moss ordered, "Let's work with the older product first. Baltimore just wants the white stuff, Norfolk probably is expecting a pound or so of the pink, and Annapolis requested three boxes of black, so a couple hundred packets per."

I tapped Mary lightly and shrugged. They both were recording this on their phones, but if these guys only talked in colors and boxes, how incriminating could that be?

We heard stuff being shoved out into the big room and plunked onto the tables. Then drills started up, and a scraping which I kind of figured would be the bulb planter. It wasn't totally dark in the office, and Alex poked me and pointed two fingers toward his eyes, like he was going to look. The next instant he was doing the military crawl to the window of the office. It had mini-blinds, which were shut, but there was a sliver of space on each side where you could potentially see out. When he arrived, he got on his knees and peered through the little opening. After a few moments, he scooted back to us and whispered in our ears. Not every word was clear, but the gist of it was, all of the crafts his mom and her team had made were being ripped or cut open, stuffed with drugs, and put back together with glue guns or crude sewing stitches. Gift baskets of lotions and soaps were augmented by packets of drugs tucked underneath the products.

I was the next one to tiptoe over there, and was really glad I had jeans and sneakers on—very quiet clothes. Jamal stood at a worktable packing a box. He slit the balsam pillow ornaments in the bottom and then inserted some of the little bags of drugs. Next, he swiped the glue gun across the opening, squeezed it shut and dropped it into the box. Many more went in followed by a couple of handfuls of the cinnamon stick ornaments. Then he cut a piece of cardboard and squished it down, apparently finished with that layer. A little farther down the table, Mr. Moss drilled holes in the bottoms of the floral arrangements. Jamal grabbed an arrangement, stuffed the hole full of baggies, dribbled a blob of glue from a hot glue gun on the plug and popped it back in. That started the layer of floral arrangements in his box.

Clayton was at the other table, concentrating on gouging holes in the larger balsam pillows with a V-shaped cutter like Mary used at the inn to sculpt fruit into fancy shapes. Then he used a melon baller to scoop out the pine needles from the pillow, and shove lots of drug bags in each hole. He had his own technique with the glue gun, sending each pass with a sweeping spread of glue sealing the pillow back up. Flinging the pillow into one of his boxes, he repeated with more, and then made a quick false bottom with the cardboard. He crammed citrus soaps and lotions in empty corners, and repeated with another layer.

Mr. Moss snagged any stray fabric items that needed closing up with a big needle and thread. Then he taped the boxes and slapped a Mountain Artisans label on them.

Both guys occasionally tossed in a cinnamon bear. Those guys were regulars at the inn, but it was crazy how many they had accumulated. I wonder if they helped themselves to extra ones when no one was around.

I needed to let Mary get over here, but I caught a glimpse of both guys start on the bags of flour from the baking kits. Each bag got the scoop, dump out and refill routine. Our of the corner of my eye, I saw Moss pack other boxes with unaltered craft items, so he did actually ship or appear to ship legit stock, too. This was a complex operation, with lots of parts. Like, who filled all those baggies with the drugs? There were so many of them.

"We'll be working until the wee hours, thanks to your unfortunate decision to travel along the Parkway at dusk. How many times have I warned you that deer are dangerous after dark? I don't know which would have been better. Hitting a deer and damaging the car, or missing it and wrecking. Either way, it put us behind."

"Look, Boss, we saved almost a hundred pounds of product, and neither of us was badly injured," said Jamal Greene.

Moss chuckled. "Yeah, I have to give you that. You two toted that stuff, what, a couple miles on foot?"

Mr. Shaw cleared his throat. "And I'd like to think our unfortunate incident just added to our little innkeeper's woes."

"For sure," agreed Moss. "We've got to have that place. We need those basements for storage, and developing that land will be money in the bank. All these little dramas you've caused have been fun to watch. Now, if the sheriff stays out of town a bit longer, our inspector can do exactly what we paid him to do. That deputy is so overwhelmed, he's happy with his first assessment of the accident, and never looked beyond the map. Why did you have 'B. Den' written on there anyway?"

Someone rattled a box. "You owed her some sticks, and we wanted to remember to give them to her."

Moss said, "She'll never miss 'em. She'll get shut down by next week."

"How are you gonna manage that?" asked Jamal.

"Oh, the inspector will use the drug connection as reason to pull her license. She'll be bankrupt before her appeal gets heard."

Mary had started toward me, but stopped abruptly. I couldn't see her face, but I felt awful for her and Gigi.

Mr. Shaw said, "Well, she's a nice lady, but I guess business is business."

"Yeah, it is," said Moss, tapping the plastic bin with the bears in it. "You remembered to toss one or two of these in each box, right?"

"Yeah," said Jamal, "I get these are part of the cutesy craft cover, but why these bears instead of just some other ornament?"

"Their scent is super strong, and should be just enough to throw the tracking dogs off if you're ever stopped."

"Or even some snooping Feds," said Jamal.

Moss nodded. "Now you're thinking. We'll need more pretty soon, but I've almost got the *chica* convinced to make them for the shop. It's just good business for her, and she's a smart one."

"Yeah, and pretty," drawled Mr. Shaw. "But, you've never noticed that, right?"

They all laughed, and I was glad I couldn't see Alex's face. Moss continued. "Okay, after Annapolis, you'll make a stop in Jacksonville, and your next stop will be back to the left coast of Florida, but not so far south as Siesta Key. You'll be up around Crystal River."

"We're getting pretty good on those Jet Skis."

"Yeah," said Moss, "I envy you guys. Back in the day, we had to bring the product on a rowboat. Nearly killed my back."

"So, you think about midmonth for the next run?" asked Jamal. "I need to be home for a few days. The wife is crabbing about chores needing to be done."

"Yeah, me too, Boss," said Mr. Shaw. "With the accident and all, we need to flesh out a new cover. Been thinking about something like 'Murray's Cabinetmaking.' We'll have signs made like we had for the painting company. People up here always want remodeling done, so it would be a logical sign to be on the vehicle. Throw a few boards in, bucket of nails, box of shingles, and the product can fill in around all that."

Moss interrupted. "That sounds fine. Do you guys smell something fancy?"

"Fancy?" asked Jamal.

"Yeah, like cologne or perfume."

"Nah, the only smell this nose twitches for is my morning coffee," said Mr. Shaw.

"Well, I detect something."

I sniffed my wrist, and felt my stomach lurch. Oh, please don't let that be what Moss smelled. The next thing we knew was the light switch to this office was thrown on, and Evan Moss stood towering over me, while I crouched by the office window.

"Well, Ms. Sanders, did you decide to stick around and photograph all this quaint exposed brick?"

I tried a snappy comeback. "Wow, that's exactly what I was doing, but I got locked in."

"So, when I step over to this desk, I won't find your compadres?"

"I'm not sure; I only speak English, sir."

"Why don't we just have them stand up? Oh, kiddies, time to come out."

Mary and Alex stood up slowly, and all of us just stood there not looking at each other. Mr. Moss paced a few steps in each direction and then stopped in the middle of the room. He held out his hand, and said "Phones and camera."

"Okay, here you go, sir," I said. "Want us to leave through the front or back?"

"You're the funny one," he said, "but a cute comment probably isn't going to work tonight, gang. We have some things to discuss, and then you three may get to continue your evening on a road trip with these nice gentlemen. Find a seat."

And out he strode, closing the door and jamming a chair under the knob. We heard the phones and camera slam into the trashcan, and then the sound of country music. Moss had turned the radio on, so whatever was going to happen next would come as a surprise, and most likely not a good one.

Chapter 25

Totally Winging It

We sat on the floor facing each other, and seemingly, no one wanted to speak. I felt like it was my fault we were in this situation, and I desperately wanted to sound like I knew what we should do. If only that were true, but I'd try faking it. "First, before too long, someone will wonder where we are."

Alex grimaced. "Nice try, but the movie just started, so nobody's going to even miss us for a couple hours."

"I know, I just didn't want anyone to panic."

"Too late," said Mary. "What should we do?"

Alex said, "I don't want to go anywhere with these goons or give in to them. Let's make noise. Someone going through town might hear us."

"Great idea," I said, "but one thing. I don't care who, if *any* of us can get free, don't look back, and just haul it somewhere for help."

Mary and Alex both nodded. "Agreed."

I slid open a desk drawer, and asked, "Ready?" I opened and closed the metal drawer over and over, slamming it shut every time. The noise made a really impressive echo off the brick wall.

Mary screeched in what sounded like Italian. I think she was trying for opera star, but she made some really awful sounds, which someone outside this building ought to be able to hear. Alex stomped on the old wooden floors and did Tarzan yells, which made me put my hands over my ears. We were loud.

In a matter of moments, Moss removed the chair, flung open the door, and in a quiet, mental patient kind of tone, said, "Enough. Jamal, do you have what I need?"

Jamal didn't look any of us in the eyes as he cut strips of duct tape from a big roll and bound our hands behind us. Then, apparently not trusting us to sit quietly, he cut some smaller pieces. Starting with Mary, he pressed that stinky grey tape over her mouth and then on mine. Whatever remained of the plan had just evaporated.

"Hold up for a minute, Jamal. The adventure story angle only will work if they rode their bikes out there, so Alex, where'd you stash the bikes?"

Alex looked directly at Moss. "Why should I tell you?"

"It might help keep Jamal from showing off his knife skills on the little one."

From out of nowhere came an impressive click of a palm-sized switchblade. Jamal pointed at Mary, and grinned.

Alex caved. "Behind the dumpster."

"Good, I'll grab those," said Moss. "Jamal, he's done yapping for now, and is ready for that tape. Gentlemen, let's load up what we've got finished, throw these three in the back, and get out to the park. Turn right just past the entrance and that'll take you in the direction you need to go. As soon as you've disposed of them, hightail it back to get the rest of the shipment, and you can leave from here. Clayton, make sure you've got bolt cutters to help you get in the entrance gate."

As soon as the three of them went to complete their tasks, Alex leaned toward me and started mumbling through the tape. First, he showed his hands to us and waggled his fingers. I couldn't quite get what he was saying, but I watched him a few more times and then nodded. He was saying to wiggle our hands to loosen the tape. Good idea. Then, he got really close to my ear and mumbled two words over and over. It took a few more times of listening closely, but I finally figured out he was saying "Magic Mountain."

Were they were going to take us to an amusement park that was closed for the night? I didn't like the sound of that, especially since Moss had used the words "throw" and "dispose" when he referred to us. I've seen stuff people heaved out of cars in rural areas. I'd be just like an old tire rolling down a slope into a ditch, my hands still bound behind me. I couldn't believe the same man who wrote me a check last week, and thanked me for all my hard work, was the mastermind of this nasty operation.

I peeked at the wall clock, hoping to slow time, but soon we were marched out at knifepoint and shoved in the middle seat of a huge new SUV. It was parked in behind the Mountain Artisans van. I wondered whose name was on *this* rental agreement! Mary was put in the middle, and Alex was on the passenger side in the same seat as us. Before we took off, Moss lashed the bikes to the roof rack, then stuck his head in, whispering in my ear. "Your hunch was right this time, Miss Snoop. Too bad it won't pay off for you."

I jerked away from him, and he shut the door. "Remember guys, these kids will have their own unfortunate accident. Do it like I told you.

I've spent too much time and money creating a strong reputation here. You will leave no way this can be traced back to me. Is that clear?"

With replies of "Yes, Boss," echoing across the front seat, Mr. Shaw put the vehicle in gear. We sped through town and out onto the Parkway. I tried to stop it, but a tear trickled down my cheek. What were we going to do? It was going on nine o'clock and not quite dark, but after eight or ten miles, we turned off the parkway and then down a side road. The only thing I could see was trees, and trees, and more trees. Wow, this area was remote, and now it was dark as midnight. Magic Mountain was in the middle of a nature preserve, with no houses or development allowed within a five-mile radius. I remembered family trips to this park. There was a Wild West show, a roller coaster and a carousel, a magic show, a petting zoo and a ride around the park on a train pulled by a steam engine. All our guests loved going there. The whistle on the engine sounded eight or nine times a day and you could hear it all through the valley. Usually it was a comforting sound, but as we bumped along a lonely dirt road, my stomach lurched in fits and starts.

I'd hoped when we finally got to Magic Mountain there would be some employees still working, but as the SUV sped into the parking lot, my heart sank again. Alex and I edged toward the side windows and peered out. The headlights flashed over what seemed to be a jillion yellow stripes marking several thousand parking spots, all empty. Security lights cast an eerie glow as a night fog moved in. I shivered and glanced at my friends. Alex was giving me a signal. I watched his knees moving up and down, then he jerked his head toward the window. If I was reading him right, we were going to try and make a run for it as soon as the doors opened. I glanced at Jamal up in the passenger seat, and hoped he trusted his taping enough not to check us as we exited the vehicle. Alex's hands were almost free. My hands were not, but I thought I could still run. I nodded and elbowed Mary. I couldn't see her hands, so all I could do was pray. This might be our only chance to escape.

Chapter 26

No Way Out

Clayton Shaw slammed on the brakes, skidded to a stop in front of the vacant ticket booth and turned off the motor. I had felt suffocated from the moment the tape was strapped over my mouth. But, trust me, when I saw him reach under the seat and come up with a handgun, I discovered you can actually scream through duct tape. I knew Moss had said we'd have an unfortunate accident, but in my heart of hearts, I thought that meant they'd dump us by the side of the road. Was this our time to die? Jamal reached into the glove compartment and pulled out another gun, a small, stubby black one he aimed like a laser pointer. I forced myself to breathe.

Jamal glanced at us in his visor mirror, and said in a singsong voice, "Okay, kiddies. Time to go to the park. Stay together."

Mr. Shaw chuckled, shoved the handgun in his waistband, and opened his door and mine. He reached under my feet for the bolt-cutters and said, "We'll throw their bikes off in the grass as we pull out. I'm starved. I hope this doesn't take long, I need some supper."

"Soon enough," said Jamal, laughing, exiting the car. Both guys pointed their guns at us and ordered us to climb out.

I swung my feet out and struggled to stand, not so much from the trembling I felt in every inch of my body, but with my arms pinned back, my balance was way off. How could I run like this? Jamal grabbed me under the elbow and pulled me along. His rough touch made me flinch, but as he tugged on my arm, I discovered the tape felt looser. My earlier efforts had made a difference. I could actually wiggle my wrists!

As the five of us neared the entrance, Jamal suddenly pulled up short. "Think it really matters if we take them in here?"

Mr. Shaw shrugged. "Not to me. We could just slip down this hill, shoot 'em, and roll them into the woods."

"Yeah," Jamal agreed, "this place is so remote, Smokey Bear wouldn't find 'em for days."

I shivered, knowing he was right. These woods were thick with towering pine trees, giant rhododendron and ferns big as tractor tires. Would anyone even guess where we were?

Mr. Shaw sighed and said, "That's the easy way, but the boss wants it to look like an accident so there won't be a chance of cops snooping around. These daredevils are going to climb the water tower and have a little swim. The redhead's won some swimming medals anyway. Might be a little chilly, but y'all just keep kickin'."

I looked at Alex and Mary, wishing a brilliant idea would come to me. Guns were not something that had ever entered my thought process. These two guys were people we'd kidded around with, cleaned their room, fed them breakfast and snacks. And now, they were going to help us die? But, I told myself, listen—even though they had the stupid guns, they were not supposed to use them on us. Our original plan would have to do. I did a little jog in place acting like I was cold, but meant it to demonstrate to my fellow prisoners that escape was still the plan of choice. I could see a crack of a smile poke out from Mary's tape. Right before a tear dribbled down over top of it.

Mr. Shaw fiddled with the impressive locks on one of the entrance gates for a few minutes. Then he opened the jaw of the bolt cutters and snapped the locks on the gate like they were toothpicks. The shape of the water tower loomed over the tracks, and I thought Alex might take off then. I was sure he knew this place like it was his own backyard. Besides outings with his family, he'd probably been here bunches of times for birthday parties, day camp visits and his volunteer work. I'd come almost every year since I was in preschool, so if we could get free, we could run these guys in circles and hopefully find a phone somewhere in the park. Or make a smoke signal, or something.

I wondered when Alex was going to make a break for it, but then it became obvious why he hadn't. Jamal had pulled Alex's body close to him, and Jamal's grip was as tight as when he used to protect a football. It was like those two were joined together. At the base of the tower, Jamal stuck the gun in the waistband of his shorts and turned the spigot on for the water tower. "We want to be sure you kids have plenty of water for your swim." Then he pushed Alex against the ladder of the water tower and pinned him there with his knee. As soon as he'd finished ripping the tape from Alex's mouth and hands, Jamal said, "Start climbing, kid." And up they went, Alex in front, Jamal prodding him along with his gun.

The water tower looked huge from down here, but was probably not as tall as my two-story house. It was round, wooden, and had a shingled roof in the shape of a chocolate kiss. There was a ladder up one side, and a long, skinny spout on the other side. A sign on the side of the tower said "Depth 15' 11."" Alex got to the top, and Jamal pushed him through a little trap door in the roof. I heard a splash, then nothing. There were a few lights on the poles near the tracks, but it had to be pretty black inside the tower.

I gave a melt-your-cold-heart look to Clayton Shaw, but he ignored it, cut Mary's tape, and pushed her toward the ladder. She was a good swimmer—we'd goofed around at the pool after school some—and both of them were athletes, so they could probably tread water pretty well. The thing was the air temp right now was probably mid-fifties and dropping. If we didn't get help soon, we might last swimming-wise, but would we stay awake hypothermia-wise?

I raised my hands and pointed my head at the ladder. Mr. Shaw nodded, slit the tape, and ripped it from my wrists, and then my mouth. When he did, I thought I could break free, but he was not born yesterday, and he grabbed the waistband of my jeans. How rude, and yet very smart. Jamal followed Mary up the ladder, and I saw him push her through the doorway in the roof. I heard another splash, and then Alex yelled, "Hi, Mary." I knew he was still alive. If we all got in there and the roof was shut, how would we ever get out?

I convinced myself to stop stressing, start thinking, and went with my first idea out of the gate. Jamal waited above me as Mr. Shaw forced me up the ladder. At about the sixth step, I slowed up just out of the reach of Mr. Shaw. Jamal said, "Keep coming little girl. We've got to get shed of y'all and be on our way out of this dump."

I nodded, and lifted my leg to the next step. "Ow," I yelled. Tears that had been hovering all night burst forth, and I uttered "Cramp" as convincingly as possible. Jamal reached his football-carrying hand down to me. As he did, I grabbed on and hauled down on his arm as hard as

I could. I heard the satisfying pop of his shoulder dislocating, and then an anguished scream. He flew past me on the way down and landed directly on top of Mr. Shaw. I took a deep breath and slid down three rungs, jumping free of the ladder for the last three. Both Jamal and Mr. Shaw lunged for my ankles, but I juked around them and ran right up Main Street of the fake western town of Mountain Village. Oh, my gosh, here was a pay phone right next to the Silver Dollar Saloon! I grabbed the receiver, thinking how much I'd like to hear Mom's or Gigi's voice. What I heard was nothing, no dial tone, no static—just a dead line.

Suddenly, the crunch of footsteps sounded on the gravel-covered street. I ducked behind a huge oak barrel on the porch of the general store. During the day, costumed townspeople played checkers seated around this barrel. The footsteps were heavy and so was the panting. Jamal ran past me. Rats, why did I ever teach him to fix his own shoulder? When I was sure I hadn't been seen, I ran in the opposite direction. Where was Mr. Shaw?

What should I do? If I went back to Mary and Alex, we might all be captured. If I left the park and tried to get to the main road, it would take forever. It had to be at least five miles away through the forest. I could see the roof of the water tower, and the little door was still open, so it was possible Mary and Alex could get out. At least they were together, so my best option seemed to be stay clear of the guys and find a phone. I inched my way along the storefronts, then slid past the fudge factory and the carousel and ran toward the middle of the park. I glanced up the hill where the tram carried people on an aerial adventure to Alpine Village. It would be great to be tucked safely in one of those little cars high above all this mess. I sighed, ducked my head and ran right into Mr. Shaw as he stepped from between the stagecoaches. "Going somewhere, sweetie?"

188

"Not with you, buster." Just like in the fourth grade when boys teased me about having red hair, I hauled back and kicked him in the shins. He yowled, hopping around in pain. I didn't hesitate, and sprinted up the hill under the tram. I was sure he'd try to charge after me, but I was a lot younger than he was, and I knew I could outrun him. He cursed at me, but my sneakers churned away up the grassy rise and I left him behind. I heard him yelling into his phone. "I had her but she got away. She's under the cable cars, heading up the hill. I'll meet you at the train."

What did that mean? I wasn't about to stick around to find out. I made it to the top of the hill and started searching for a phone. Each building, from the restaurant to city hall, was locked tight. I heard an odd sound, like a creaky door in a haunted house. I was near the platform where the train dropped off passengers in Alpine Village. Peering down the tracks, I couldn't see anything coming. However, I felt vibration under the platform. *Something* was on the tracks, and as I squinted in the darkness, I couldn't believe my eyes. Coming up the hill, pushing a metal handle up and down like a see-saw, Clayton Shaw and Jamal Greene were running the hand car that the train repairmen use.

I leaped off the platform and ran for the only set of doors I hadn't tried—the big wooden ones that swing open to let the cars into the Rabbit Mine. I loved the Rabbit Mine when I was a little kid. You rode in a mining car deep into a hill and watched a show where rabbits sang and mined for carrots. It was kind of silly, but cute if you were five. I shoved against the doors, and even though they were braced at the top, they gave way just enough for me to slip between them. To my surprise, inside it wasn't pitch dark. A soft glow from the security lights made it bright enough for me to run deep into the mine. As I passed a bunch of support beams, I skidded to a stop. A phone was attached to one of the beams! I picked it up, heard buzzing, and then a voice said, "This is Ralph. Who is this?"

"My name's Emily Sanders," I said, words tumbling out so fast it probably sounded like I'd swallowed helium. "I'm trapped inside Magic Mountain."

"You're in there now? The park's closed."

"Sir, my friends, Mary Carnell, Alex Ortiz and I were kidnapped in Winton and brought here. Please call the police."

"Miss, this here's a maintenance phone."

"I'm sorry to bother you," I said, wondering how I could get this guy to understand me. "I'm in the Rabbit Mine and some bad men are chasing me."

"Have you been drinking, miss?"

"No, sir. I'm only fourteen."

"All right, miss, I'm reporting this, but stay on the line. Okay?"

"Yes, sir, but one more thing. The two guys who are chasing me have guns, and a third one, Evan Moss, is still at Mountain Artisans on Front Street. "

When he came back on, Ralph asked, "Are you kids together?"

Big tears started to roll down my face as I remembered seeing Alex and Mary shoved into that little bitty doorway. "No, I'm in the mine, but we got separated. They might still be trapped in the water tower."

I heard the murmur of voices echo down the mine. Jamal and Mr. Shaw were in here!

"Ralph, I've got to go. Thank you!" I hung up the phone and broke into a run, trying not to turn my ankle on the uneven gravel. I whizzed past carrot stalactites and fake rabbits that, during the day, danced and played and dug for jewels. In the eerie night light, they looked like soldiers with big ears guarding a cave. I wished the rabbits were singing right now to muffle my steps, which rumbled off the walls like drum beats.

The tunnel seemed to go on for miles, but finally I saw an exit sign over the big wooden doors. I kept running at full speed as the guys shouted, "There she is! Get her!"

Hoping to force it open, I smashed into one of the doors, but it barely budged. Pushing again, I squeezed through the crack between the doors. Moonlight glowed and I felt a soft night breeze brush my face. Then a powerful hand latched onto my ankle, which was the only part of my body still in the tunnel. I squirmed and twisted and pulled my foot right out of my sneaker. I was free!

In the next instant, I was stunned by the loudest firecracker I'd ever heard. Firecracker? Of course not, those were gunshots. I didn't wait to see if the men were able to shoot their way through the doors. I just ran for my life.

I raced down the hill on the train tracks. The night air was frigid. How many minutes could Mary and Alex survive in that water? I know we agreed whoever got free had to go for help, but why had I ever suggested that? I'd left them and there still was no sign of help. After this long, it might be past the point to do them any good at all.

A little way down, I heard the clang of metal on metal. What was that? I didn't want to take a chance, so I jumped off the train tracks and scrambled down the hill the way I'd come up. Unfortunately, it was still pretty dark, and except for that metal noise, ominously quiet down here. I had hoped, by now, to hear sirens blaring, or big spotlights flashing from patrol cars. It was just a short while ago, but had Ralph actually called the police? What if he thought it was a prank? Keep going, I told myself, just find my friends.

I headed for the last place I'd seen them, the water tower. If the guys were out of the mine, they might be on the way there too. I definitely wanted get there first, but I just hoped I wasn't already too late. I cut through the village square, sped up the ladder to the water tower roof, and pulled my flashlight from my pocket. At the little opening into the tower, I called, "Alex? Mary?"

There was no answer, just the sound of water lapping against the wooden walls of the tower. Humans don't stay conscious long in cold water. I knew I had to look, had to find out, and I forced myself to breathe. I gripped the last step rung, held on, and peeked over the edge of the opening. The light on top of the tower cast a little glow on the water rippling below me. The beam from my flashlight shone on the flat, still water and confirmed they weren't in here. No floating bodies. Relief swept through me so fast I nearly lost my footing. Wait, what was that? There were little metal rungs spaced up the inside of the tower. This was like the inside of a silo. If you could make it to the side walls, and had any strength left, you could get out. Where could they be? As I clambered down, a thought flashed through my brain. Maybe they'd left the park and were able to flag a passerby on the highway, or they'd broken into one of the buildings here to hide until the park opened in the morning. As I neared the bottom rung, I wondered if *I* should find a hiding place?

Too late, as the moment my foot hit the ground, someone grabbed me from behind, threw an arm around my neck, and pressed a hand over my mouth. A voice whispered in my ear, "Don't make a sound. I'm here to help you."

I recognized the voice. Jim Adams! I elbowed him and he grunted in pain but his grip held fast. "I know you're scared. I'm an undercover government agent. Trust me. Don't yell, okay?" As I nodded, he released his hand from my mouth.

"I *knew* you weren't an Audubon guy," I grumbled. "Apparently, all you've been doing is lying to us, and now I'm supposed to trust you?"

He reached into a pocket, pulled out his cell phone and badge. Then he dialed the phone. "Jim Adams, ATF here. I've got one of those kids, Emily. Can you verify my identity to her?"

I took the phone. "Hello?"

Instantly, a voice said "Emily, this is Deputy Bennett. We're about ten minutes out from your location. You're with Federal Agent Jim Adams. He heard about your call for help on the police scanner, and was closer to you than our nearest officer. He'll keep you safe until we get on scene."

"Okay," I said, in a doubtful tone.

"We've contacted Gigi Baird, and she confirmed you, Mary and Alex were together this evening."

"Yes, but then we were kidnapped."

Agent Adams pointed to the phone and pushed the speaker button. "Emily, tell us, who are these guys?"

"Jamal Greene and Clayton Shaw are running drugs out of Mountain Artisans and we discovered it. Evan Moss is the ringleader, and he wanted them to kill us but make it look like an accident in the water tower. Alex and Mary had to get in first, but before they could shove me in, I escaped."

"That was a gutsy move, young lady. Deputy, we can't take this bunch lightly. Can you dispatch a patrol car to pick up the Moss guy? That shop's on Front Street. Now, I need that backup."

"They're due any minute sir. You'll be able to hear them coming."

"We're counting on it, Bennett." He took back his phone and pushed the "off" button. "So, the last time you saw your friends was at the water tower, correct?"

I nodded, suddenly realizing my bare arms felt like two popsicles. I untied my jacket from my waist and put it on. "But they're not up there now."

"Those guys don't know that, so this is probably where they'll come, thinking you'd be trying to save your friends."

"So, we're just going to sit here?"

"Well, no," he said, "I want you to stay put, hidden from view, while I do a quick scan of Main Street. If I don't find them, then hopefully we'll find them scaling the tower."

I opened my mouth to object when the whistle sounded. Before either of us could speak, we heard a man's voice say, "Forget the tower. Head for the train."

Now I knew what I'd heard coming down the hill. Less than the length of a basketball court away from us, Jamal and Clayton seesawed on the railroad handcar toward the train. A train that most likely thought it had been put to bed for the night. Who woke it up?

Agent Adams whispered an order. "This way."

We moved away from the tracks, crossed through the center of the park, ran the whole length of Main Street to the other side of the village and skirted behind the jail. There, on a short side spur, sat the big black engine, with steam hissing. The whistle blew again. Not twenty feet away from us, the Mountain Artisan guys stood on the handcar. They began shooting at the engine like they were in a cowboy movie. We ducked behind a pile of coal, and Agent Adams pulled out his gun. We heard police sirens in the distance, and he gave our position and status over his phone.

Suddenly the area in front of the engine blazed full of light. The big headlamp of this old beast had come alive, blinding our two captors. They turned away, knelt down, and began reloading.

"Stay here," Agent Adams instructed as he vaulted from our hiding place. He shouted, "Federal Agent! Drop your weapons!"

Clayton Shaw and Jamal Greene were having none of that. They jumped up and whipped around, shooting like crazy people or guys who didn't use guns every day. Their random shots rang out in the vicinity of Adams, but honestly, they were crooks, not hired marksmen.

Agent Adams fired back what were probably considered warning shots because I could see they weren't really aimed at anything but the sky. But in the dark, the guys couldn't see that little fact, and it apparently freaked them out. Their guns went silent. The combination of the train light and Agent Adams had basically frozen them in place. The sirens of police cars in the parking lot were loud enough now to hear over the steam of the engine. It was obvious the guys were outdone on all fronts. They dropped their guns to the gravel and threw up their hands in surrender. I had never seen actual handcuffs slapped on someone, but let me say, that moment filled me with joy.

Minutes later, Agent Adams and two deputies with guns drawn turned their attention to the engine. One ordered, "Lights out!"

Instantly, the light went dark. Then the whistle blew two long, one short, and one long sound. "Sir," said one of the deputies. "That's the signal they sound at a crossing."

Agent Adams held up a hand to the deputies and stepped purposefully back toward the engine. "Stand down in there."

I held my breath as he pointed his gun at the steps of the engine. A fakey-deep voice said, "Don't shoot."

Agent Adams relaxed his stance, gestured toward the train, and said to me, "I'm guessing this one looks familiar?"

Alex, greasy, smudged up, with a weird piece of fabric wrapped around his forehead, stepped down from the engine. Grinning from ear to ear, he waved a big wrench and yelled, "Take that, you suckers."

I sprinted over and gave him a hug. "Was the inside of the tower terrifying?"

"It was very wet and cold, but with what you did, we weren't in there long."

"Oh, I'm so glad to hear that. It didn't feel like the right thing to do."

"It was, for sure. You had no way of knowing about the ladder thing on the inside. We almost didn't see it. And, Mary almost checked out. She nodded off and I had to keep shaking her until we discovered those rungs to escape." He pointed to a bump on his head. "Then when we climbed down the outside of the water tower, those steps were so slippery I skidded over the last few and banged the concrete pad pretty hard. I guess Mary saw all the blood, wrapped me up in—"

"Hey, that's her scarf."

He nodded. "When I came to I had this thing around my head. As soon as I could get over here, I started fiddling with the engine."

"Why?"

"When I realized those guys were after you, I thought I'd try and make some noise to confuse them, *and* maybe wake somebody up. Hearing this whistle at night should have alerted someone."

"How'd you get it started?"

"I've watched the boilermaker guy whenever I volunteer out here. You know me and machines," replied Alex, pointing the wrench at me. "I bet you'll never tease me again about tools. *And* I had help." He nodded toward the coal car.

Standing up, sooty from head to toe, was Mary. I screamed and ran to the steps of the coal car. "You're alive!"

"I am," she said as we hugged, then high-fived. "But I freaked with him knocked out, so I thought I'd try and find you. I started up the hill but the trouble was, things were so crazy and there were noises like gunshots coming from on top of the mountain. I didn't know where to go. Then Alex groaned. I sprinted back and helped get him here. He was super focused and put me to work shoveling coal."

I stared at her, thinking that's what's cool about having a friend. Just when you think you know everything about them, they amaze you. "Good job, missy. Apparently, you can use a shovel as well as a spatula. Who knew?"

Agent Adams stepped toward us. "You kids were remarkable tonight. But you *all* were in grave danger."

Mary looked at me. "Hey, why is the bird guy here?"

Jim Adams grinned. "So that's what you call me. Not as bad as some things I've heard." He cleared his throat. "Sorry I couldn't have told you earlier who I was."

"Sorry?" said Alex. "So, when are you gonna tell us?"

"I'm an ATF agent, Alcohol, Tobacco, and Firearms. I'm up here investigating a major moonshine operation. It starts in the back corner of the Baird's Den property, and extends quite a ways into the land trust."

"Ah," I said, nodding, "now all your weird wandering around and fake bird tracking makes sense. So, what about Mr. Moss?"

He shook his head. "He's a whole new kettle of fish for law enforcement. It appears you and your friends have exposed a drug operation that might include much of the eastern U. S. That's a good thing, of course, but you three will most likely have to give statements, and possibly testify."

"We'll do that, but our phones and camera with all the evidence are in the trash can at Mountain Artisans. Can you call someone?"

"I'll do that right now. Then you should contact your parents." He moved away from the three of us.

"What a mess," Mary said, wringing out her shirt. "I dressed to sleuth, not go swimming for my life. My hiking sandals are floating around in that stupid water tower, and my feet are shredded from running on this gravel." Shivering, with her teeth chattering, she leaned against the train. "But, we're alive, right?"

"Pretty much," I said, smiling. I gave her my sweatshirt and glanced at the dried blood on my arms and ankles. "I didn't realize it, but I'm pretty wrecked, too. At least I still have one shoe."

"And my gram has her inn," said Mary. "I think we saved Baird's Den."

"So, Emily," said Alex, "when we were busy firing up the engine, where were you hiding out?"

"Hiding out?" I started counting on my fingers. "After I escaped from the water tower, I caused bodily harm to a thug, ran *up* a mountain, broke into a locked mine, convinced a maintenance guy named Ralph to call for help, and only lost one shoe doing it."

"Slacker," said Alex, grinning, as we met Agent Adams and walked toward the parking lot. "Hey, if anyone wants an interview, I'm available. That would be by appointment only, of course. There will probably be a movie deal coming. Maybe *now* you'll have actual news to write about for the paper."

"Yeah, maybe I will." I watched my friends examine their scrapes and bruises, thinking about how lucky we were. The warmth from the engine wrapped around me. Even with the smoke from the coal, it smelled good up here. Fir trees, night jasmine, and sweat; the only thing missing was the smell from a steaming hot cup of hot chocolate in Gigi's kitchen. That was where I needed to be, so I could stir in the most special ingredient, a stick of cinnamon. I was wondering how soon we'd get there when Agent Adams interrupted by handing me his phone.

I took it and said, "Mom? Dad?"

ACKNOWLEDGEMENTS

Huge thanks to: Chris Klein, Dana Arace, Penny Noyce and Barnas Monteith of Tumblehome Learning. Also, much appreciation to my critique group of amazing children's writers: Joan Hiatt Harlow, June Estep Fiorelli, and Betty Conard.

Continuing gratitude for their encouragement goes to my Aunt Yarda (Ervin), and cousin, Chris Ervin. And, to my North Carolina native & devoted Tar Heel husband, Mont Hedrick, I send more love and thanks than anyone will ever know. Without him, 'Sneaky' would never have made it to THE END!